WITCH UNDERCOVER IN WESTERHAM

Paranormal Investigation Bureau Book 3

DIONNE LISTER

Dionne Lister

Copyright © 2018 by Dionne Lister

ISBN 978-0-6483489-7-9

Print Edition

Cover art by Robert Baird

Content edit by Becky at Hot Tree Editing

Line edit by Chryse Wymer

Proofread by Mandy at Hot Tree Editing

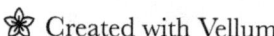 Created with Vellum

For my cats, Lily and Izzy. You helped make me the cat lady I am today.

CHAPTER 1

I'd done it, but regret nipped at my heels with the enthusiasm of a hyperactive puppy.

Life-drawing classes had seemed like a good idea at the time. Olivia, my first girlfriend in Westerham, had thought so too, and she'd signed up with me. We stood at our easels in our second lesson, charcoal scraping against paper. The model, as naked as the day he was born but rather hairier, lay on his stomach atop cushions piled in the centre of the rustic barn conversion.

I guess I didn't regret joining the class so much as where I'd positioned myself in relation to the model—directly behind. Today's model looked to be in his early sixties, and some things were, um… saggy. It was taking me awhile to adjust to this new reality. Actually, seeing anyone nude was a new reality. I hadn't dated anyone in months.

Our teacher, Mrs Valentine, waddled over. She was an

enthusiastic older lady with a purple bouffant, bright-red lipstick, and a vibrantly coloured Mumu that rippled and flowed behind her when she walked. What she lacked in height, she made up for with her loud voice. "Oh, very nice, Lily. Although, you might want to change this line." She gently bumped me out of the way as she took control of my feeble attempt at drawing. I bit my lip as she calmly rubbed out the offending curve between the legs and redid it to her satisfaction. "There. That's better. Lovely." She smiled and moved to the next student.

Olivia leaned over and whispered, "Oh my. Nice ball sac. Mrs Valentine sure knows what she's doing." She tried holding back, but I heard her quiet snort.

I snickered. I had so chosen the wrong angle. Why hadn't I planned better? I'd have to remember for next time. At least the lessons seemed to cheer Olivia up. Her fiancé had been killed a month ago in a PIB arrest gone wrong. My brother had shot him but only to save me. I'd struggled with survivor's guilt since then. I felt like I'd contributed to Olivia's fiancé's demise, and every time I saw her struggle, everything came back as if it had happened yesterday. Although everyone kept telling me it wasn't my fault, I couldn't help thinking it.

Maybe saggy balls were good therapy for both of us. Yep, things must be bad.

A phone trilled loudly from another room. The barn conversion was divided into four rooms: the large main area with high ceilings and exposed timber beams where art lessons were held, then Mrs Valentine's office, the supply storeroom, and the toilet.

Mrs Valentine shuffled quickly to answer the phone in her office. She raised her arm and waved it in front of her as she went. "I'm coming. I'm coming. Don't get your knickers in a twist." She finally reached her office and shut the door.

I whispered to Olivia, "Do you think she realises whoever's on the phone can't hear her until she actually answers it?"

She shrugged. "I have no idea. You'd best get a move on. You're only half finished." She turned back to her easel and shaded the curve of the model's lower back.

"You're not half bad at this drawing caper."

She smiled. "Thanks. I'm really enjoying it, much more than I thought I would."

Happiness surged through my chest and curled my lips into a grin. If anyone deserved to be happy, it was Liv. She was one of the nicest people I'd ever met.

I bit my lip and started drawing our subject's arm. The trick, apparently, was to look at what you were drawing more than the paper. And from this angle, everything was foreshortened. I'd be happy if I could just tell it was a person when I was finished.

Just as I was becoming absorbed in the work, Mrs Valentine came out of her office. Her smile was gone, and her face was flushed. "I'm so very sorry, class, but I have to leave —bit of a family emergency. When you're finished, please stack the easels in the storeroom. Henry darling, do you mind locking up?" She pulled keys out of her pocket and gave them to the model.

"Will do, Ida. I'll bring them by tonight." His Irish accent was delivered with a deep voice. He winked at her. Hmm, it was like that, was it? I quietly snorted. But why was I laughing? A seventy-year-old was getting more action than I was. Life could be so unfair.

Mrs Valentine winked at him, then smiled. "Good man. Bye, class. I'll see you next week." At the door, she put her fingers in her mouth and screeched a loud, sharp whistle. My eyes widened when a red fox—yes, a fox—arrived and trotted away with her.

I shared a glance with Olivia. "Um, is that normal?"

She laughed. "Not really. Some people have foxes as pets, usually rescued animals who choose to stay. Actually, she's the second person I've met who has a pet fox."

Ooh, I was so jealous. Foxes were super cute. If you don't believe me, just watch a YouTube video of one playing —they're the perfect combination of cat and dog. My glee turned to a frown. "They're classed as pests in Australia. The government baits them." They were so adorable with their bushy tails and pointy ears, but they killed a lot of native animals. Why couldn't they be herbivores so they'd be allowed to live happily in Australia?

"Hmm." Olivia tilted her head and regarded her work. "What do you think?"

"It's quite good, actually. Much better than mine." Mine would be going in the bin when I got home.

"Thanks. And thanks for asking me to come. I think I've found something I really enjoy." She smiled.

"Glad to be of service."

The lesson ran for another fifteen minutes, and then it was time to pack up. We put our easels in the storeroom, then collected our stuff. On the way out, I stopped to thank the model, who was still without clothing. Okay then. I swallowed and tried to make sure I had a normal expression on my face. I also didn't look down. Nope. I stared at his face, his smile crinkling his brown eyes at the corners, until I thought about his saggy balls, and I blushed. Could he tell what I was thinking? My gaze fled, but not too far. It wandered down to his chest, where he had a heart-shaped mole, just above his nipple. I was totally doing this talking-to-a-naked-person thing.

"Thanks for today, Henry."

He smiled wider and put his hands on his hips, as if he was trying to draw my attention down there. "My pleasure. How did it go?"

Not. Going. To. Look. How could he stand there so... so... *naked* without a care in the world? "Ah, my drawing sucked, but Olivia's was quite good, actually."

"Good to hear. See you next time, ladies." He winked, then turned and bent over to pick up some cushions. My mouth dropped open. And I'd thought the view before was confronting. I wanted to shut my eyes and look away, but you know how it is when something surprises you so much you just can't believe it and your brain shuts down? Me. Right. Now.

Olivia pulled my arm and broke the spell. Thank God. We turned and hurried out. My boot toe caught on the bottom of the door frame, and I tripped, grabbing onto Olivia to save myself.

She laughed. "You idiot. It's just a naked person."

"I know. But can't he put his clothes on when the lesson's over. I didn't know where to look, and then, well, who bends over naked in front of people they hardly know?"

"Someone who's comfortable in their skin."

"Yeah, well, I can't unsee that. I'm glad you're so okay with it. At least only one of us will be having flashbacks. Oh God, what if I have one during sex? My life is ruined."

"Ha, you have to meet someone to have sex; I'm pretty sure. When was the last time you went on a date?"

"Yeah, don't remind me."

"What about Mr Tall, Dark, and Cranky?"

She'd gotten to know William a little in the last few weeks, and her assessment was accurate. I cleared my throat. "What about him?"

"I see the way you two look at each other."

"What, angrily?" I smirked.

She grinned. "Yeah, sexual-tension angry."

"Oh, would you look at that. There's your car."

"You can change the subject, but you can't avoid me forever." She cackled an evil laugh and unlocked her car.

"How's the studying going?" Olivia was doing an online course on policing. It was the first step to joining the PIB. She was supposed to have moved in with Angelica and me, but her parents had insisted she stay with them for a while.

She agreed, knowing how worried they were since her fiancé had been killed, although they didn't know the exact circumstances.

"Great, actually. I'm almost halfway through. Another five weeks, and I should be done. I have to study tonight, hence why I can't come out to dinner with you guys. Have dessert for me."

"The things I do for my friends." I sighed dramatically and got in the car. Angelica, my brother, James, his wife, Millicent, and Beren, William, and William's model sister, Sarah, were going out to dinner for Millicent's birthday. It was the first time I'd been able to attend her birthday, and I was chuffed. I was finally part of a family again for the first time since my parents had disappeared when I was fourteen. It wasn't quite the same, but it filled the empty space that had been in my heart for so long. I had people again, even if they were mostly witches.

Olivia turned on the radio, and we sang along to Taylor Swift's "Shake it Off."

I smiled. Yep, I had peeps. The best witchy and non-witchy peeps ever.

❦

It was 11:00 p.m., and it was dark. Finally. Not that I didn't like summer and daylight, but it was weird to have a late dinner in bright sunlight. I was stuck in the middle of the back seat, again, between Angelica and Beren. William drove his Range Rover, as usual. His sister sat in the front passenger seat, which wasn't usual, since she was often working abroad. My brother and Millicent had taken their own car. We'd had a delicious dinner, and true to my word, I'd also had dessert. Chocolate mousse. Yum. My stomach strained against my jeans, and I couldn't wait to get home and rip them off.

Sarah turned around and looked at me. "How are the art lessons going?"

"Good, thanks. Well, they're fun, but I'm not very good. That would be the more correct answer." I laughed.

She shrugged. "Hey, everyone has to start somewhere. You'll get better. Is it like landscapes and stuff?"

Beren grinned, then coughed. "Our wild Aussie girl is drawing nudes. Isn't that right?"

Sarah's eyes widened; then she nodded. "Okay, I wouldn't have expected that, but good on you. The naked form is truly beautiful."

I blushed. "Kind of. We've only had old people pose so far, but that's fine; I'm not there to perv. It's taking me a while to adjust though. It's kind of awkward sometimes, and I have to force myself not to laugh at some weird thought, or I'll look like an arsehole."

"Maybe they could get some hot young man there for you." Beren tapped his chin with his forefinger, pretending to think. Then he thrust his finger in the air. "I know! Will would be perfect. I hear he has nice tight buns."

I snorted, then burst out laughing, as did Sarah.

William scowled. "Very funny, idiot. Although, you do speak the truth about my buns."

Sarah leaned over and felt his bicep. "B has a point, Will. You could earn some extra cash."

He blushed, the scarlet inching up his cheeks to envelop his ears, kind of like on a cartoon when someone eats a hot chili. Wow, I never knew it actually happened.

I grinned. "I have the perfect red pencil I could use to colour in your face." Angelica and I laughed. William narrowed his eyes at me in the mirror. I smirked.

A flash of something caught my attention in the headlights. Oh my God! "Stop!"

William had reacted just as I shouted. He must have noticed what I had at the same time. The tyres screeched. A small thud sounded. My stomach plummeted, and then the car stopped. We'd hit an animal. I was sure of it.

William unbuckled and jumped out. I didn't want to see the damage, but I had to. What if whatever it was wasn't dead? Beren had opened the door and was already running to the front of the car. I unbuckled and followed him. *Please don't be dead, animal.*

I swallowed as I rounded the bonnet. A small furry body, about the size of an Australian sheepdog, lay on its side in the middle of the road a couple of metres in front of the car. Beren had his hands on its head. William stood watching, his arms limp by his side. When I reached them, I could see it was a fox. Oh no.

"Beren, is it…?"

He looked up at me, and the fox blinked. "No. Just give me a minute. I'm going to heal it." If Beren wasn't my favourite person before this, he was now. Looked like witch healing wasn't just for humans.

William bit his lip, and deep lines marred his forehead.

"Hey, are you okay?" I put my hand on his arm, and he looked down at me. "It wasn't your fault. In fact, it was probably my fault for distracting you. I'm sorry."

He shook his head. "I should've been paying better attention. But even if I had been, it would've been hard to avoid, as it ran out from the bushes at the side of the road where it's dark. It wasn't anyone's fault. Not really, but, yeah, I feel bad."

Angelica called out from the car. "Maybe put your hazards on, Will."

"Yes, Ma'am." He turned back to the Range Rover.

I knelt next to Beren and studied the fox's face. There was blood on its pointy snout, but its eyes were open and staring at Beren, and there were definite up and down chest movements indicating it was breathing. Thank God.

Beren slowly removed his hands. "Done. You're one lucky fox. If anyone else had hit you, you would've died."

There was something around its neck. I was about to reach out and see, but then I remembered that as cute as this fox was, it was a wild animal and would probably bite me. "What's that around its neck?"

The fox wriggled, preparing to stand, but Beren mumbled something, and it lay still, its eyes opening wider, showing the whites. It was scared.

Beren reached down and ran his fingers around the fox's

neck. "It's a collar. Here's a tag." He leaned down. "It says, 'Knight. If found call 7724886340.'"

"It's a pet?"

"Seems to be."

"I'll call the number." I pulled my phone out of my jacket pocket just as William rejoined us, Sarah in tow. I dialled while Beren explained to them what was going on.

The phone rang a few times before it went to a message bank. "Well hello!" an enthusiastic and familiar woman's voice almost shouted. "You've reached Ida Valentine and Naked Art Studio. Please leave a message after the beep, and I'll return your call post-haste. Toodle pip!"

A mini explosion detonated in my brain—*think quick, Lily*. Out of all the people it could have been—how much should I say? "Ah, hi, Mrs Valentine. It's Lily Bianchi from one of your classes. Um, your fox is out on the road, and I thought you should know. We'll drive him to your place now, just in case you're wondering where he is. Bye." Gah, I hadn't left my number. But she had my number from art classes. Okay, all good.

I turned, and Beren had moved the fox to the side of the road.

William looked at me and folded his arms. "What did you just do?"

"That was my art teacher. It's her fox. I actually saw him with her this afternoon. She had to run off to deal with some family emergency, and he went with her. We need to take him home so someone else doesn't run him over."

"You're not putting a fox in my car."

I gave him an incredulous look. "Why not?"

"Foxes smell. I don't want to stink up my car."

"Oh, for goodness' sake. It's a five-minute drive to her place from here." Her studio sat on the back of her large block, and her 1850s house was near the front, a pretty cottage garden bridging the gap.

The fox yelped. "I can't hold it much longer, and your car is still in the middle of the road, Will." Beren had a point.

I took charge, and if William wanted to be cranky with me, let him. It wasn't as if I wasn't used to it, and guess what? I hadn't died from his ire yet. "Let's go. Beren, can you keep it calm and put it in the back of the car?"

Beren looked at William's thunderous face, then back at me.

"If you don't do it, I will," I said as I strode towards them. "You don't scare me, buddy." I stopped in front of William and tipped my chin while wearing the fiercest "I dare you" face I could muster. He raised his brow but didn't protest further. I bent to gather the fox into my arms, but Beren lifted it instead.

"I got this, Lily. Just get in the car." Beren shook his head.

I followed him to the Range Rover. "What's the point of you healing him if we're just going to let him get run over again, huh?"

"Good point." Sarah patted my shoulder.

While the guys put the fox into the back, Sarah whispered to me, "I can't believe you did that."

"What do you mean? Stood up to him? I do it all the time."

"No, I've seen you do that before." She giggled. "I mean, made him put a fox in his car. He loves that car. He must have it bad."

Have it bad... for me? Whilst there were times I wished that were true, I knew it wasn't. He put up with me because he had to, and there was no way I was going to let my brain lead my emotions in that direction. I was in a pretty good place right now, and romantic heartbreak was something I could do without. "Nah, he's just a bit scared of me." I grinned and hopped into the back seat, and she got into the front.

I directed William where to drive and every now and then looked in the back to check on the fox. "It's okay, Knight. We'll get you back to Mummy soon."

The fox whimpered. I wrinkled my forehead. "Beren, would it still be in pain, or is it upset to be bound?"

"I unbound it. It seems calm. If it does any damage to anyone, I can heal them."

Angelica chuckled. I stared at her and shook my head. She was always laughing at stuff like that. Talk about a dark sense of humour, or maybe she was a sadist or something.

"That's the driveway, just there."

William put his blinker on, and we turned right. The house was about thirty metres in, and all the lights were off. *Argh, don't tell me she's not home.* The fox looked out the window, sat up, and growled. It pawed the glass, then screamed. I clamped my hands over my ears. Yikes. Who knew foxes could make that noise. Sheesh. And William was not going to like it scratching the glass.

Where was Millicent when you needed her? She could have communicated with Knight. "I'll just check if she's home."

Beren opened his door and got out. "I'll come with you."

"Thanks." I wouldn't have said I was scared, but Knight's reaction had my hackles standing on end. Something wasn't right. Or maybe I was jumping to conclusions. Maybe the fox hated being in a car and was desperate to see his owner?

It was dark, but William kept the headlights on, illuminating the small porch and front door. An old-fashioned bell hung to the right of the door. I dinged it a few times and rapped on the door for good measure. She was old, and judging by how loudly she spoke, she was probably a tad deaf. We waited a minute, and I knocked again.

Nothing.

Beren and I looked at each other. He pressed his lips together, then said, "I don't like this. I'll check round the back."

"Her studio is down there. I'll come with you."

Beren turned and gestured to everyone in the car that we were going round the back. We walked to the driveway and followed it to the garden, then took a paved path down to the barn conversion. Cricket chirps and frog croaks pulsed into the cool night. The new moon gave only enough light to hint at the landscape, creating menacing shadows out of harmless plants. Goosebumps shimmered along my arms. *There's nothing wrong, Lily. It's just a normal night. Mrs Valentine is probably at a friend's or something.*

I squinted, trying to see better as the land gradually sloped down towards the barn conversion, which was a hulking shadow looming about twenty metres away. I stubbed my boot toe on an uneven paver and shot forward before regaining my balance.

Beren laughed. "Are you okay?"

I couldn't help laughing at myself either. "Yeah, I'm fine." The creepiness was still there, but laughing helped things seem normal. "Um, how come neither of us has made a ball of light?" This was a spell I knew, and if I knew it, he surely did.

"I have no idea. We're a couple of geniuses, aren't we?" Beren lifted his hand, and a glowing blob appeared in his upturned palm.

"Thanks. That's so much better." Now I wouldn't kill myself on the path.

We reached the barn, Beren's globe the only light. I leant my forehead against the glass of the French doors and tried to see inside. "I can't see anything. Should we knock?"

"May as well."

I rapped my knuckles on the glass and called out. "Mrs Valentine. Are you there? Hello? It's Lily, one of your art students." Nothing. I tried the handle, but it was locked.

I turned to Beren. "I'll try calling her again." I dialled, and just as before, it rang through to a messaging system. I hung up and shook my head. "Now what?"

"Why don't we see what Angelica thinks?"

"Sounds good." If anyone could sort things out, it was the super-organised bossy witch who was second in charge at the Paranormal Investigation Bureau. While she scared me at first, I'd gotten to know her over the past couple of months, and even though she was still scary at times, she had a good heart under the stern exterior.

Back at the car, Sarah and the fox were sitting on the ground as she patted its back. Knight watched me, and while his ears were forward, on alert, he'd calmed down. I approached slowly and knelt in front of him. "Can I pat you?"

He tilted his head to the side, and I tentatively reached out. He didn't snap or growl, so I figured it was okay to proceed. I rubbed his chest. Oh my God, the fur was so soft! That was unexpected. Although he was a wildish animal, Mrs Valentine probably groomed him, and people wore fox fur coats in the 70s, so I supposed it showed foxes had soft fur. I hadn't really thought about it before.

Ooh, I had an idea. I stood, opened the back door, and poked my head in. "Ma'am, can I call Millicent? We didn't find anything unusual, but this whole thing feels wrong. Mrs Valentine left with her fox this afternoon, and I can't imagine she would let him just wander off far from home and then not answer her phone when he was missing."

"I agree, Lily. Make the call, please. In the meantime, hop back in the car, and Will can take us home. We'll take the fox overnight. He can sleep in the laundry. I have a dog bed he can use."

She'd had a dog? I wondered if she was mushy with dogs or just as strict as she was with humans. Interesting, but a question for another time.

I hopped in, and Beren helped Sarah put Knight in the back. When we were all buckled in, Will pulled out of the driveway and turned right. I turned to look at Knight. He was staring out the back window, and once the house was out of sight, he hung his head, then lay down.

"It's okay, Knight. We'll find out where she is. Don't worry." His ears pivoted towards me, but he didn't turn his head. I frowned. Poor fox.

It was time to get some answers, so I called Millicent, and she agreed to meet us at Angelica's.

When we arrived at Angelica's quaint English cottage, which was actually quite a large home, with five bedrooms and three bathrooms, Angelica and I bade everyone good-night. The back of the Range Rover opened automatically at the push of a button. I shook my head. Were rich people too lazy to open their own boots? As funny as I found it, a little voice inside me called out, *But I want a self-opening boot, and a Range Rover would be nice, but in yellow.* Okay, so maybe I was a bit jealous.

"Hey, Knight. Time to get out. You're going to stay here tonight, and as soon as we find Mrs Valentine, you can go home."

He whined, then blinked before hopping out and trotting to the front door. My mouth dropped open. I looked at Angelica. "Did you see that? He understood."

She shrugged, and Knight looked back at me from the

front door as if to say, "So? What's so weird about that?"

"Of course he understands, dear. He's a familiar."

"A witch's familiar?"

"Yes. They're quite common."

Huh? Wow, so Mrs Valentine was a witch. I supposed I should have expected this was a thing, because all the fictional books I'd read with witches had them. I'd just thought it was a cliché, like having a broom and a pointy hat. "But you don't have one, neither do Beren, William or Sarah. Are James's dogs familiars?"

"No, they're regular dogs. Maybe they just don't have time for one? They need even more attention than regular pets. They're more like best friends, and they can talk to their witch in images sent to their mind. They understand language too." Her gaze floated over my shoulder to some place I couldn't see. Her voice held a wistful tone. "I used to have a familiar—a beagle called Roger. He died many years ago. Familiars live a bit longer than others of their species, but they still don't live nearly as long as we do, unless you were to get a parrot or elephant, for instance." She turned abruptly and unlocked the front door. Knight and I followed her in.

An elephant? I shook my head. Who the hell had room for an elephant? Maybe circus witches had them. Were there circus witches?

Knocking came from the reception room—the locked room in a witch's home or business where witches could pop in and out from. Angelica opened that door while I took Knight into the cosy sitting room. I sat on one of the

Chesterfields, and he lay on the blue Persian rug at my feet, curling his red bushy tail around himself, like a cat. I stroked his head and along his back. So silky.

Millicent and James walked in. James had his arm around her. They were so cute.

"Long time no see." I smiled. "Thanks for rushing over."

"Not a problem." Millicent came and sat beside me, her white trench coat still on—they must have just made it home after dinner when I called. She was the only person I knew who could wear that much white and still be clean five minutes later. Angelica walked in and joined James in taking a seat opposite us. Hmm, make that two people. I'd never seen Angelica with even a hair out of place. I looked down at the thumb-size oily stain on my black pants from dinner. You couldn't take me anywhere.

"I'm going to talk to him now. This may take a few minutes." I sat back and gave her room so she could look the fox in the eye. He sat straight, lifted his head, and swivelled his ears forward. She stared at him, nodded a couple of times. The fox tilted his head to the side. Listening?

Knight growled but made no move to attack. As subtly as I could, I slid to the side, further away from him.

"It's fine, Lily." Millicent turned to me. "He's telling me about what happened, and he's angry. I just need another minute." She turned back to the fox.

Millicent nodded and patted Knight. He whined and pawed the rug.

"Okay, sweetie. We'll figure this out. While we do that,

you're going to stay here, and Lily will take extra good care of you. Okay?"

He nodded. *What?*

"Does he understand English?"

"Yes, he does, although I communicated to him in pictures just then. He understood what I said. He's also asked that you take him for walks while he's here. He doesn't need a lead. And he likes raw chicken, rabbit, cheese, and nuts." Millicent smiled at Knight.

Wow, you learned something new every day. "Cheese and nuts? What about a glass of red?" I snorted.

The fox looked at me, cocked his head to the side, and I swear he rolled his eyes.

Millicent smirked. "He said he prefers white."

I giggled. "Nice. We have a fox with a sense of humour." I looked at Knight. "We're going to get on just fine. And don't worry; we'll find Mrs Valentine."

His eyes definitely looked sad, so I leaned over and rested my hand on his back. He leaned into it. My chest ached. Poor guy, and poor Mrs Valentine.

Angelica, sitting up straight, her hands clasped in her lap, cleared her throat. "So, what did he say?"

"During the art class this afternoon, the one Lily was at, Ida, Mrs Valentine, received a phone call from her nephew, Isaac. He'd learned from his father, Mrs Valentine's brother, that Mrs Valentine had cut them out of her will, while the Westerham Art Society was getting everything."

"Was the art society in the original will?" I asked.

"Knight doesn't know. He only found out that much

because Ida, Mrs Valentine, was rambling about it on the way to her brother's house. Apparently she called her brother and niece and nephew 'leeches.'"

"Are her relatives witches?" I wanted to know where we stood when it came to investigating this. The more witches involved, the trickier it was going to be. Not that it was really my job. They'd asked me a few times to come work for the Paranormal Investigation Bureau (PIB) on a permanent basis, but I didn't want to answer to the head of the whole operation—we'd gotten off on the wrong foot, and I didn't trust him, not to mention, I loved photography. That was the only full-time job I wanted. But this was interesting, so I couldn't help but get caught up in it.

Millicent looked at Knight, then answered, "Yes, her relatives are witches."

I nodded. "So what happened when she got there?"

"They wouldn't let Knight stay inside—they put him in the back garden. There was lots of shouting. A couple of hours after they got there, just after dusk, Ida sent Knight a mind message, telling him to go home, that she was going to be a while. She sounded fairly calm, according to Knight, so he did as she asked, but he said he was still worried. He didn't trust her brother. On his way home, just as he was about to cross the road, he felt a sharp pain in his chest, so he wasn't paying attention. That's when he ran in front of William's car." Millicent took a deep breath and rubbed her belly. "He said he can't feel her anymore. He thinks she's dead, or, at the very least, being shielded."

Knight lay down, put his head on his paws, and whimpered softly. I knelt next to him and whispered, "Is it okay if I give you a hug?" He gave a small, sharp whimper that I took to mean yes.

I placed one arm around his fluffy neck, and he snuggled against me and sighed. Who knew foxes could be so human? Please don't be dead, Mrs Valentine. If she had been murdered, so many people would miss her. Everyone in the class loved her. I hadn't gotten the chance to know her well enough for that, but who wouldn't like such a creative, vivacious, and happy person? She brought so much energy with her—if she was in the room, you knew it.

Millicent turned to Angelica who pursed her lips, then cleared her throat. "Before we do anything, we should call the local hospitals and her brother. I'll pop over to headquarters when you leave and get Phil onto it. Depending on what we find, we'll reconvene tomorrow morning in conference room one. She's not a missing person yet, and we're not going to panic over a few missed phone calls and the worries of a fox, no matter how *adorable* he is." She raised an eyebrow at me.

What had I done?

Knight's shoulder muscles bunched under my hand, and he growled quietly. Seemed like he didn't agree with Ma'am's assessment.

I squeezed him gently. "I know, buddy, but we'll get to the bottom of it. There's protocol we have to follow."

Millicent looked down at the fox, her face sombre. She looked back to Ma'am, nodded, then yawned. "Okay, Ma'am. Sounds like a plan."

James stood. "Time to get you home, Mill. You and the baby need some sleep." James held out his hand and helped her up, although at four months and this being her first, she wasn't showing yet. Which was probably a good thing. Once whoever was hunting my brother and I found out she was expecting, Millicent and the baby would become targets. James planned to restrict her time in public when she was finally showing. Maybe I could come up with a camouflage spell? Hmm, something to think about.

"I'll come by tomorrow and have another chat with Knight, just in case there's anything he's forgotten or that I think of. I'll see you in at headquarters tomorrow, Ma'am."

Millicent waved, and James said, "See ya, little sis."

Angelica stood and walked with them to the reception room. I stayed on the floor and waved. "See you guys later."

Every week, my magic sense seemed to be getting stronger. The faint tingle of their magic tickled my scalp as they left. Before now, unless I was right next to the person making a portal, I couldn't feel it. I gave myself a small smile. Maybe I'd get the hang of this being-a-witch thing yet.

Angelica returned. I gave Knight one last pat, then stood. "Have we got food for him?"

"Not really, but there's some cheese in the fridge. Give him some of that, and on my way home from the Bureau, I'll get some fresh meat."

"Cool." I turned to Knight. "Come with me."

His paws made barely a sound as he followed me into the kitchen. I'd read somewhere that foxes could retract their claws like cats. Another reason foxes were amazing. I grabbed the sliced cheese out of the fridge and pulled out a few slices. "How much do you want?" I held up one flat square. Knight shook his head. I held up two. Nope. I held up three. He nodded. I laughed. This was beyond awesome. I put the slices on a plate and set it on the floor. "I'm just going to have a shower. I'll be back down soon."

Knight bowed his head and ate. I jogged upstairs, grabbed my PJs, and had a shower. When I was clean and changed, I returned downstairs. Knight was curled up on the rug next to the Chesterfields. He blinked at me.

"Hey, puppy. I know you're a fox, but foxes are a type of dog, and puppy seems appropriate. Is that okay?"

He shrugged. Yes, this was my life now. Foxes who could understand English. "Okay, so, would you like to stay here, or would you like to sleep in my room? There's a rug there, or I could find that dog bed Ma'am has."

He opened his mouth and kind of bark-squeaked, then stood and trotted to me.

"I'm going to take that as a yes to sleeping in my room. Do you want the dog bed?"

He nodded.

Hmm, where would she have put it? I checked in the linen cupboard, then the closet under the stairs with no luck. There was probably a spell I could use to find it, but I didn't know it. I went upstairs to my room and grabbed my phone, Knight padding behind me. Sitting on my bed, I called Angelica. "Hi, Ma'am."

"What is it, Lily. I'm just in the middle of something?"

How unusual. I sensibly kept my thoughts to myself. "Sorry to bother you. Just wondering where the dog bed is? Knight wants to use it."

"Oh, of course. Where are you right now?"

"In my room."

"Okay. Hang on a second."

The bed appeared on the floor at my feet, and I jumped, my heart hammering. Jesus. "A little warning would be nice."

She laughed. "Got to keep you on your toes."

"Thanks... for getting the bed, not the surprise."

"You're welcome, dear. Now I have to go."

"Bye." The line dropped out. I wanted to ask her about Mrs Valentine, but she sounded like she was in such a hurry, and I didn't want to get chastised, plus it was probably better to get news in the morning because if Ma'am had found her alive and safe, she would have said. There was no use giving Knight bad news right now. It could wait until morning.

Once Knight was settled, I hopped into bed. He was curled up so his tail rested against his face. "Sleep well, puppy. And whatever happens, I'm here for you."

He opened his eyes and gazed at me before closing them again. I wished I knew what he was thinking. Was talking to animals something I could learn? I'd have to ask Millicent tomorrow.

I closed my eyes. *Please, universe, can we find Mrs Valentine safe and well tomorrow?* The universe owed me, dammit. I just hoped it was listening.

CHAPTER 2

T he next morning, Angelica and I ate breakfast together in the kitchen. Angelica had bought some rabbit steaks for Knight, and I placed one on a plate on the floor, but he shook his head, then lay at my feet while I ate breakfast. I guessed he was sad and missing his witch.

After breakfast, we headed to Angelica's reception room and straight to the Bureau, Knight in tow. He stayed by my side as we strode along the sterile hallways. Angelica led the way into the conference room, and I shut the door behind us.

The usual crew was there—my brother, Millicent, William, and Beren, but there was one face I wasn't happy to see. Drake Pembleton the Third, the big boss at the Bureau. His dark hair was neatly trimmed and parted on one side. He ran his fingers down his green tie and gave a curt nod. "Good morning, Angelica, Miss Bianchi."

"Good morning, Drake." Angelica took the seat to his right.

I'd never thought about it before, but he was named after a duck. His full name sounded really posh and formal —like his voice—but underneath it all, he was basically just a fowl. I bit my tongue to stop from laughing. "Good morning, Mr Pembleton." I kept my voice as neutral as possible and sat at the far end of the table away from them, next to Millicent. I'd never think of him the same way again.

Knight followed me and lay under the table at my feet. Millicent leaned down and stared at him. He made some squeaky noises, and she nodded, then sat up again. "He says to tell you thanks for breakfast, but he's not hungry."

"Thanks." I bent to look at the fox and gave him a rub behind the ears. "I know, Knight. We'll find her. I promise." Whether she'd be alive, I couldn't promise. I sat up and sighed. Why did bad things have to happen so often?

Drake Pembleton cleared his throat. "Welcome, all. I'm calling this meeting to order." He looked at his watch. "I have another meeting in fifteen minutes, so I need to make this quick. Angelica has reported that Mrs Valentine isn't in any of the local hospitals, and her brother says she left his place shortly after Knight. He told us she said she was going home. In my opinion, she hasn't been missing for long enough for us to get too excited."

Knight whined, and Millicent nodded. "He says that he can't feel her, which, we can all agree, is serious."

Drake sniffed. "Well, yes, hence this meeting. I don't want to waste our resources, but I have agreed that agents Bianchi and Blakesley will head over to Mrs Valentine's brother's today to interview him and find out what occurred last night. They will report back to Angelica, and if she feels the need to investigate further, I will decide from there."

Ma'am's eyes narrowed ever so slightly, and only for a split second. Hmm, so the old Drake was pecking away at her unshakeable façade. Why was he trying to assert his authority? Maybe he was worried she'd come after his job one day. I'd be worried if I were him: she was damn good at her job.

Drake ran one hand down his tie again. "I'd like Agent DuPree, Millicent, and Lily to take the fox and search Mrs Valentine's property. If you find anything, relay it to Angelica, and she can update me this afternoon." He stood. "You're all dismissed." He turned and gave Ma'am a nod. "Angelica."

"Drake."

He took one step and disappeared. As soon as he was gone, Ma'am gritted her teeth before schooling her features to their regular nonplussed expression. Was that whole exchange sexist, or was that my imagination? He'd given the "agent" honorary to all the men but called all of us women by our first names, although in my case, that was fine, since I wasn't an agent. Maybe I was just being sensitive, but I didn't think so.

James stood. "Ma'am, we'll report back to you as soon as we've finished."

She gave a slow nod. "Thank you, James."

James turned to William. "Okay, let's go." They walked to the door.

Huh? "How come you guys aren't travelling?"

William turned his head as he reached the door. "We don't have the coordinates for her brother's reception room."

"Oh, right. Have fun."

William almost smiled. His lips made it to a straight line. Okay, so maybe I was putting a positive spin on it. They left, and Millicent stood. "Okay, let's go. I'm driving." She pulled a set of keys out of her bag and jingled them.

Beren and I stood. I tilted my head down to look under the table. "Come on, Knight. Let's get you home and see if we can find your mum." The fox stood and stretched. I turned to Angelica. "We'll see you later, Ma'am."

She stood and joined us at the door. "Use correct protocol. I don't want *anyone* suggesting any evidence we find isn't important enough or wasn't collected in an appropriate way." Was "anyone" supposed to mean Drake?

"Yes, Ma'am," Beren answered.

"Lily, go home and grab your camera. See if you can pick up anything from last night."

"Yes, Ma'am."

Her brow wrinkled. I turned and followed Millicent and Beren out the door, Knight at my side.

Ma'am's voice drifted down the hallway behind us. "Be careful."

She didn't have to tell me twice.

CHAPTER 3

Millicent parked on the driveway just inside Mrs Valentine's property line. "I don't want to disturb any evidence if another car's been here since you last night." She reached into her small, camel-coloured handbag and pulled out two pairs of rubber gloves, giving one to Beren. "Lily, can you just stick to taking photos, please? If you need to open any doors or if you see something suspicious, let me or Beren know. Don't touch anything."

"Okay. I can manage that." I smiled. Sounded simple enough. Now I just had to hope I wouldn't see any dead bodies through my viewfinder.

We all got out of the car, Knight included. He leapt down and started sniffing. I took the lens cap off my camera —which I'd managed to magic to myself—and got to work. Beren was studying the driveway as he ambled towards the house, and Millicent went straight to the front door and knocked. I guessed we should check if she was home. Wouldn't that be funny? I could see us ferreting around for ages before she came out and asked what we were doing. Unfortunately, no one answered the door.

I thought for a minute about what I needed to ask, then lifted my camera. "Show me Mrs Valentine from yesterday afternoon." Down the driveway, near the house, a yellow Mini appeared. It was an original model, not a modern one, totally cute and totally something I could see Mrs Valentine driving. She stood there, door open as she waited for Knight to jump in, the fox in mid-leap. I took one photo, then got a close-up of the number plate. I studied her face. She looked more annoyed than worried, her lips pressed together and one hand on her hip.

I put the camera down and called out to Millicent, who was making her way down the driveway to the back of the house. "I've got her number plate. Should we call Angelica and get her to run it through the system, see if her car has been towed in the last twenty-four hours?"

She stopped and turned to face me. "We can do that later. Let's keep looking around, get a feel for what might have happened, if, indeed, anything has happened."

"Okay."

She spun and kept on down the driveway. I lifted my camera again. "Show me if anyone was here last night."

The scene through the lens darkened to night-time, and there were two shadowy figures on the porch. I walked closer. Just as I thought: Beren and me. Well, that wasn't going to help.

"Hey, Lily." Beren straightened from his examination of the ground. "What kind of car does she have?"

"A Mini, one of the older ones from the sixties. That's when they were around, wasn't it?"

"Around then. They started production in 1959 and finished in 2000."

"Impressive. You sure know your stuff."

He grinned. "I do. And thanks for the info."

"Any time." I smiled and returned to my camera. I'd have to be more specific this time.

"Show me if anyone was here last night other than Beren, William, Ma'am, Sarah, Knight, and me." I bit my lip while the power vibrated my skin, and I waited to see if my magic was that precise.

The scene had changed—Beren and I had disappeared, but someone else was standing on the porch with his hand on the doorknob. A white hatchback sat in the driveway, but the Mini was nowhere to be seen. Was the person trying to break in? There was even less light than when Beren and I had been here, so did that make it later? I panned the camera to the sky. The moon was hidden, but it looked almost at its zenith. I couldn't remember its position when I'd been here. Was this before or after we'd come by?

I snapped the car and number plate, although it was almost unreadable in the dark. Then I trod carefully to the front porch—I could hardly see anything, and there were no headlights to help me this time. Lowering the camera wasn't an option, in case the image disappeared and I couldn't get it back.

"Hey, careful." Beren's British accent came over the top of his shuffling footsteps.

I kept my camera to my face. "Sorry. Can't see."

"Yeah, I noticed. Do you need a guide?"

I couldn't help but smile. "I should be fine, just try and keep out of my way."

"Yes, Ma'am."

I tuned him out and concentrated on making out the person on the porch. I stepped up the two steps and stopped just behind him. I edged around him. His profile was in shadow, but I could tell who it was, and it made sense.

Henry.

He was probably just dropping off Mrs Valentine's keys. I snapped some shots anyway and tried to see if he was holding her keys. It didn't look like it, and I couldn't tell if they were in his pocket. Had he just used them on the door? His hand was around the knob, but I couldn't tell whether he'd turned it. Had he gotten in?

I lowered my camera. "Show me if Henry got in." I lifted the camera. Daylight and the empty front porch filled my lens. Damn. I took a fortifying breath.

Knight trotted past and down the driveway. I had to find her for him, if for nothing else. She was his everything. Sadness swelled up through my chest, to my throat, and pulsed at my eyes. I blinked. *No crying on the job, Lily.*

I turned my camera off, stomped off the porch, and followed the fox down the driveway to the barn conversion.

Knight sat next to the front door and stared at me. He then stood and touched his nose to the door.

"You want to go inside?"

He opened his mouth in what looked like a grin.

"Okay then, buddy. But I don't have a key. I'll see if Beren or Millicent can help."

Knight turned and walked to a pedestal that held a Grecian-style concrete pot with a silver-leafed ground cover spilling over the sides. He touched it with his nose.

"Is there a spare key hiding there?"

He nodded. My mouth dropped open, although how I could still be surprised was beyond me. I should have expected it. In fact, if he had opened his mouth and actually talked, it should come as no great shock. I felt as if I was on an episode of *Skippy the Bush Kangaroo* or *Lassie*. Hopefully there were no wells around, because someone always got stuck, and we didn't have time for that.

I approached the plant and ferreted around under the leaves. My fingers caught something cold and hard. I lifted it out. The key! Yes! "Thanks, Knight. Good job." I stroked his head, then went back to the door. I was just about to put the key in the lock, but then I realised I was technically tres-passing, and stupid Drake was out for blood, if Ma'am's warnings were anything to go by. I needed to do this by the book.

"Just a minute, Knight. I just have to okay this with Millicent." I headed back to the rear of the house, where she was standing with her eyes closed. After a minute of me waiting quietly—I didn't want to disturb her since she was obviously working, not having a power nap—she opened her eyes and smiled.

"Yes, Lily?"

"Knight wants to go into the barn, and he showed me where the key was. Can we go in?"

She bit the side of her bottom lip. "Hmm. Well, technically, Knight lives here, and he's invited us in, but that wouldn't stand up in a human court. I'll have to check with Angelica."

I pulled my phone out of my back pocket and dialled Angelica.

"Hello, Lily. How's it going over there?"

"Nothing much so far, but Knight wants us to go inside the barn. He showed me where the key was. Is it okay, or do we need a warrant?" I had no idea what protocol was. Everything I knew came from watching TV or reading mystery books, and I was sure some of it was wrong.

"Can you put Millicent on, dear?"

"Yes. Hang on." I handed the phone to Millicent. "She wants to talk to you."

She put the phone to her ear. "Hi, Ma'am.... Yes.... Okay, then. Will do. Bye." She pressed a button and handed my phone back. "I just need to speak to Knight and ask him why he wants us to go in. If it's a valid reason, we can use it. It's a tricky situation, but the PIB should allow it, since familiars are treated as reliable sources of information in these matters." She bent down and gazed into the fox's eyes.

Well, that was good to hear. After the way Drake had spoken down to Knight, some witches obviously didn't like familiars or pets, for that matter. How could you not like animals anyway? They all had their own personalities and were loving and cute. Well, domesticated ones anyway. I wouldn't risk trying to cuddle a lion or panther, even though it was tempting. I was always envious of those people on Facebook videos who had their own big cats. That would be so cool, although they probably ate a lot, which meant cleaning the litter would be a b—

"Lily?"

"Oh, sorry." *Focus, idiot.* I hit my palm to the side of my head.

"Are you okay?" Millicent stared at me.

I smiled. "Yeah, just drifted off into the ether for a minute. Sorry."

"Let's go. Knight showed me a picture of a young man going through her desk drawers. He doesn't like this man, says he's using Ida for something, although he doesn't know what. He just knows his intentions aren't what Ida, Mrs Valentine, thinks they are."

I handed Millicent the key, since she was the real agent here, and followed her and Knight back to the barn. Millicent reached under her PIB jacket and pulled out a gun. Whoa, where had she been hiding that? I supposed as an agent, she would have to have a gun, but she was a petite, sweet-looking woman, as in, I wouldn't have thought her out of place sitting with the Queen eating scones. Seeing her holding a gun was quite the shock. *Shame on you, Lily, stereo-typing your own sister-in-law.* She did look quite badass with it, though.

Birds happily chirped, and a willy wagtail landed near me, swaying its little rear end from side to side. The cuteness was at odds with the tension building inside me as Millicent cautiously entered the barn, Knight by her side. My heart rate kicked up as I waited for her to turn on the lights and have a quick look around before I went in. If anyone had been hiding in there, or if, God forbid, Mrs Valentine was dead in there, I didn't want to get in the way or see something I didn't have to.

A minute later, she returned, slipping her gun back in the holster at her side. "All clear. You can come in and take some photos."

"Great. Thanks." I turned my camera on and stepped inside, to the main room where we did art classes. I shivered. It was cold with nobody in here to warm it up, and obviously she'd had heating before to make sure the naked model wasn't freezing. I walked to the far wall, where I'd have a view of the whole room, and turned.

So, what should I ask my magic for? I bit the inside of my cheek. Hmm. "Show me Mrs Valentine with the young man Knight told Millicent about." I panned my camera from the left side of the room to the right. There, on the green couch at the far end. Oh dear. I stepped closer, even though I didn't want all the details. She was smiling and lying naked underneath the model from the other night, Henry. I pulled a face, my bottom lip contorting in distaste. Why did I have to see all the naked people? I heavy sighed and clicked, but only because it might be important. Not that I could see how it would be, but you never knew.

I lowered my camera. Why did my magic have to play up and show me that? Unless I wasn't specific enough and the universe misunderstood and thought I meant someone younger than her? Maybe I had to be age-range specific? Well, whatever, I wasn't going to find him in this room. Best to go to the desk where Knight had seen this man before.

Her study was a cosy room with bright-orange carpet, a timber desk, and black-framed paintings on the white walls. The paintings were of all different subjects, from nudes to a garden scene replete with pond, ducks, and swans.

With my camera poised in front of my face, I said, "Show me the young man going through Mrs Valentine's desk drawers." I did not want the universe to misunderstand drawers, so I had been careful to say "desk" in front of it. I shuddered. *No more naked people, please.*

The light outside the window disappeared, replaced by darkness, and the only light in the room was her desk lamp. A young man was sitting on her chair, his broad shoulders hunched over as he went through her bottom drawer. I snapped a shot from near the door, then stepped closer to photograph his hands in the drawer. After that, I panned the camera up and took a close-up of his face. He looked to be maybe thirty and had quite a handsome face with scruffy light-brown hair and striking brown eyes. His fringe almost covered one eye, and his lips were full and set in a pout. He obviously wasn't finding what he was looking for.

There was something familiar about him, but I couldn't figure it out. I was pretty sure I'd never seen him before, but my memory was terrible, and I tended not to stare at people when I was out and about. Wouldn't want to make eye contact with a stranger by accident. But there was nothing to say I hadn't come across him in Westerham.

While he wasn't stunning, he was attractive enough that I should have remembered seeing him, especially since I hadn't been in the UK that long and hadn't come across too many men that piqued my interest. I knew I was picky, but sue me. That was probably why I was still single, but I didn't feel like dissecting my fussiness now.

What was he after? She was an art teacher. What could she possibly have that someone would be trying to steal? A rare and expensive piece of art, maybe? Argh, we had a long way to go with this. Who knew? Maybe she'd turn up this afternoon after a day of hanging out with Henry. Oh, that's what we needed to do—call Henry. His number had to be somewhere around here, although we didn't even know his last name.

I hurried outside and almost bumped into Beren, who was just reaching the barn. "Someone's in a hurry. Did you find something?"

"Yes, kind of, but I just thought of something. She has a boyfriend, if you can call him that, or maybe a man friend? He's too old to be a boy." I grinned. "Anyway, maybe she's at his place or they went for an overnight stay somewhere?"

"And she didn't tell her familiar? That doesn't make sense."

I thought about my friend Michelle and her cat. Whenever we were going anywhere, she told her cat where we were going, as if it could understand and even cared.

Maybe it was a pet-owner thing. "Maybe it was a last-minute thing, and she came back here to tell him, but he was with us."

He quirked his mouth to one side, then scrunched his nose. "I doubt it, but it's a possibility. Do you happen to have this guy's number?"

"No. His name's Henry, but I have no idea what his last name is. Maybe Knight knows."

"Let's go find out. We'll come back and lock up after we talk to Millicent, just in case the information is in Mrs Valentine's study."

Argh, this wasn't going well. We'd spent half the morning investigating and didn't seem to be any closer to finding her. I hoped Will and James were having more luck. I guessed we'd find out this afternoon.

When we went around to the front of the house, the door was open. "Is Mrs Valentine back?" I asked.

"Not that I know of. And her car's not here."

Millicent appeared in the entryway. "I unlocked the front door with magic. I haven't been looking for evidence. I don't think we can push things that far, but Knight wanted to come in and have a look around."

Today hadn't gone well, but maybe it was salvageable. "Can you ask him if he knows the name of the young man?"

"Did you find something?" she asked.

"I have a photo of him going through one of her drawers. I've never seen him before, though."

"Okay. Can you give me your camera, and I'll show

Knight?" She reached out, and I handed her the camera. She turned and went back inside. Beren and I followed.

Two doors led off the hallway. We walked past those and headed for the door at the end, which opened to a lounge room. Millicent kept going through a wide opening to the kitchen-cum-dining-room. Her sharp intake of breath made me start. She'd unexpectedly stopped walking, and I bumped into her back.

"What's wrong? Is it the baby?" I hurried to stand in front of her, but then I halted too. *Oh no.* "Beren, quick!" I ran to kneel at Knight's side. His eyes were closed, body limp, tongue hanging out of his open mouth. I placed my palm on his chest as Beren dropped to his knees next to me.

I concentrated and held my breath so I wouldn't miss anything if Knight breathed. But nothing happened. His warm chest didn't move. Beren placed his hand on him too, and I waited, fighting back tears.

Beren shook his head, his eyes sad. "I'm sorry, Lily. He's dead."

"Isn't there anything you can do?"

"I'm a healer, not a miracle worker. What you want is impossible, Lily. I would if I could." He looked down at Knight and gently ran his hand over the fox's head.

Millicent let out a sob, and it broke me. The wave of tears I'd tried to hold in surged from my eyes and flowed down my cheeks. I hugged the fox. "I'm so sorry, buddy. Poor baby. I'm sorry we didn't get here in time."

Plastic crinkled near my head. I looked up. Beren was collecting a sample of food in a small bag. "Evidence."

"Someone poisoned him?"

"That would be my best guess." He sealed the bag. "Let's get out of here. We need to talk to Ma'am, find out what we're going to do now. I'd like to set this up as a crime scene, but since we weren't supposed to be in here…"

Millicent sniffed and ran her forearm across her face, wiping her eyes with her sleeve. "We'll figure it out. He did ask if we could go in, and this *is* his home."

Beren went to her and put his arm around her shoulders. "Are you okay?"

She shook her head. "He was such a beautiful boy." She rubbed her tummy.

"Should I take some photos? This is a potential crime scene, isn't it?"

Beren looked at me. "Mr Pembleton may not see it that way, but why take chances? That would be great, thanks, Lily. I'll pop back and notify Ma'am about what's happened, see if I can get a team here to collect any other evidence; then we'll take Knight for an autopsy. I'll be back soon."

He popped out, and I gave Millicent a hug, sadness sucking the energy right out of me. What kind of cruel bastard would poison such a gorgeous animal? My chest tightened, and my heart hurt. I didn't get to say goodbye, tell him again that I would find Mrs Valentine.

Now we'd likely never find out who that young man was. And maybe that was just the way he wanted it. Had this mysterious man killed Knight?

I released Millicent. Knight looked lonely, lying there next to his bowl, his red fur shiny, belying the fact he was dead. I sat next to him again and stroked his fur. "I promise you, we'll find who did this, and we'll find where your mum's gone. Sleep well, little one." Another tear fell and dropped into his fur. I looked up at Millicent. "I'm not going to stop till we catch the bastard who did this."

"I'll be with you the whole way, Lil." Her gaze hardened, and I knew that whoever had done this was going to pay. Big time.

I turned on my Nikon and asked, "Who was the last person to feed Knight?" It was dark—whoever had come here to feed Knight hadn't turned on any lights, but they were at his bowl, bent over and dropping mincemeat out of a plastic bag.

I trained my camera on the person's face, and although it was dark, there was enough light to see it was a man. I could barely make out his features. He had thinning dark hair and was maybe fifty-five or so? It was hard to tell in the dark. He had a Roman nose, but there wasn't enough light to distinguish his eye colour.

The glint of something on his hand caught my gaze. A thick gold band on his left hand flattened to a square at the top. I clicked some more photos, then slowly walked backwards to get a shot from further away, showing the man putting food into the dog bowl. I stood without taking my eyes from the camera, checking for anything in the room with a clock or device showing the date, to prove it was from last night, but there wasn't anything. Well, this was the only clue we had. I hoped it wasn't a false lead.

"I've got what we need, I hope."

"Okay." Millicent bent and gently laid her palm on Knight's side. She bit her bottom lip, then stood and looked at me, her cheeks wet with tears. She whispered, "Let's go to headquarters."

She disappeared. I wasn't far behind.

CHAPTER 4

W e were back sitting around the PIB
boardroom table. For someone that didn't
work for them full-time, I was sure spending a
lot of time there. Angelica sat to the left of Drake. He had
his elbows on the table, fingers steepled in front of his face,
and he kept poking his nose with the tips of his joined
pointer fingers. He irritated me when he squished his nose
like that. It was kind of gross. I was hoping his fingers would
slip and he'd painfully scratch inside his nostril, and by the
side-eyes Ma'am was giving him, she was wishing for something similar.

He turned his assessing gaze on me, and panic gave me
a shot of adrenaline. I checked my mind shield. Phew. It was
there for once. What did he want with me?

"So, Miss Bianchi, you were there when the fox died?"
His tone was very headmasterish and firm. Where was he

going with this? Was he trying to get Millicent and Beren in trouble, or was he trying to find a way to undermine Ma'am's case?

"I was outside, but we all found him. He asked—"

His hand shot up, palm facing me. "You've answered the question sufficiently. Thank you."

I couldn't help my eyebrows rising, and when I looked to Ma'am, she had her poker face on. I needed to take lessons.

"Agent Blakesley, please tell me what happened at your interview with Mrs Valentine's family."

"Her brother admitted they fought about their lack of inheritance, but he swears she left of her own volition, and she was alive and well when she left. She had been upset, he said, and she'd left her phone there. We have it in our possession. He didn't know where she went after that, but she did take her car."

My brother put up his hand. "I'll just interject here. He was telling the truth. We asked him if he, his son, or daughter had hurt her in any way, and he said no. There were no lies in his statement."

"That you could find." Drake tilted his head to the side.

James's cheeks flushed. "That I could find, but I'm never wrong." His dark gaze never left Drake's. *Go, James.* My brother wasn't going to back down. Another reason to love him. He always fought for what was right, and he never gave in to bullies.

Drake turned his head towards Ma'am, his neck stiffly straight. He gave her a snooty down-the-nose gaze. "Until the fox has had an autopsy, I'm not taking this case any further. There's no evidence of foul play with the family. If the fox has been poisoned, we'll look into it again."

"But—"

Millicent put her hand on my arm, and I looked at her. She shook her head. I wrinkled my brow. Why didn't she want me to say anything?

"You have something you'd like to share with us?" Drake stared at me, his eyebrows drawn down.

"Um, actually, no. I think we've covered everything."

"Good. In that case, I have another meeting to get to. We'll reconvene when the autopsy is finished. In the meantime, Agents Bianchi and DuPree, I need you with me to cover the Preston case."

James and Beren stood. "Yes, sir," they chorused.

Ma'am's face stayed serene, but I saw the telltale twitch of her arm muscle that suggested she was gripping her chair's arm. What was going on—a power struggle of some sort? Maybe the PIB bosses had realised Ma'am was much better at this than he was, and he was trying to derail her cases? And yes, I got that I was making a massive leap over a chasm of guesses, but what else could it be? Unless the PIB really was trying to cut costs, but if they were, stocking expensive Prestat chocolates in the cafeteria—Angelica had brought them home once and told me where they'd come from—was not the way to do it.

My brother and Beren stepped through their doorways a second after Drake. Ma'am whispered something and waved her hand in an arc. "It's safe to talk. I've created a bubble of silence. Come sit closer. I think a cosy powwow is in order."

Millicent sat on Ma'am's left, and Will and I sat opposite them. His subtle, yet sweet, cologne wafted over to me. Mmm. He smelled good. I resisted the urge to lean across and sniff his neck. I reached under the table and pinched my thigh through my jeans. Pain radiated over my skin. Now was not the time to be pining after Agent Crankypants. He'd made his non-intentions quite clear in the South of France after we'd caught Camilla and Frederick. He'd been hurt badly and wasn't going there again.

Click. Click. I blinked. Will was clicking his fingers in front of my face. I started.

"Earth to Lily. Come in, Lily."

I turned my head. He was leaning towards me. His grin warmed my tummy. How strange to see him happy, yet how nice. "Hi," I said and smiled.

"Ahem." Angelica's raised brow punctuated her smirk.

I blushed, and Will snickered. "Sorry. I was just think-ing." Damn hot cheeks. Shame I didn't wear make-up all the time. Some extra-thick foundation should take care of my embarrassments when they occurred.

Angelica clasped her hands and rested them on the table. "I want to know what your thoughts are before I decide how we're going to play this. After listening to James, Will, and Beren before this meeting, I know there's some-thing going on, and that Mrs Valentine is probably as dead as her familiar. We're going to keep investigating this while we await the autopsy, but we'll do it quietly. I don't want to go against my boss, but even he can't stop a necessary inves-tigation. He'll have to come around eventually, and I'm sure he will, but in the meantime, we're letting clues and avenues of investigation run cold. It won't happen under my watch." She lifted her chin, her eyes shining with defiance and determination.

Go, Ma'am.

"So, to recap, her brother, niece, and nephew claim to have seen her alive and well, a fact that is corroborated by James and Will's questioning. Her familiar has potentially been poisoned, and Lily has taken photos of an unknown man rifling through her study desk, a man her familiar didn't like, and before you could get a name, the fox was killed."

Millicent nodded, her shoulders sagging. "That sums it up, Ma'am."

"I have a question, Ma'am."

"Yes, Lily?"

"Can we question her male friend, Henry? I don't think he did it, necessarily, but maybe he knew what other things were going on in her life. He may even know who that man in the photo is."

Angelica reached down beside her chair and brought up her black handbag, then placed it on the table. She slipped her hand in and pulled out a mobile phone. "Mrs Valentine's phone is locked up in evidence, but I had James back up the phone and put all her contacts into this phone. Tim is quietly looking into all her recent calls for clues. Based on the large number of phone calls she's been getting from the Westerham Art Society, we'll need to sit down with each of the board members as well."

Will leaned forward. "Ma'am, do we know how much she's worth? We asked her brother, and he said she owns her home and a couple of paintings he thought were worth something, but he wasn't sure. I think we need to figure out whether her net worth was enough to justify kidnapping or murder. As far as her family goes, I don't think they would've killed her for her money, even though Isaac, the son, was upset about being cut out of the will. The brother owns his own home as well, although they're not rich."

"Tim's already looking into that. It's still a possibility. But I want the members of the art society interviewed, separately. You'll have to wait until tomorrow afternoon to start, unfortunately. Drake will have James tied up until then."

Millicent shrugged. "Why not get Dana to help? She's just as good as James in the truth telling."

Ma'am jerked back, then looked at Will, who gurgled as if he was being strangled. He looked like he'd swallowed a fly and seen a ghost at the same time, white-faced and mouth twisted. He took a deep breath and forced his expression back to sternness. "I don't think that's a good idea, Millicent." His voice was strained, almost pleading.

Who was this woman, and why didn't he want to work with her?

Millicent's hand flew to her mouth. "Oh, I'm so sorry, Will. I forgot." Ma'am looked aghast, like "how the hell could you forget" aghast.

"Baby brain. I really am sorry." She bit her bottom lip and shrugged.

I hated being the only one out of the loop. I wanted in,

dammit. "Who's Dana? She couldn't be that bad, surely." Whatever she'd done must have been bad to cause this reaction. Was she another Snezana psycho?

"None of that's important." Ma'am wore her no-nonsense expression, and her back was ramrod straight. "She's an exceptional agent. We'll wait until tomorrow afternoon, but if there are any more delays, you'll have to work with her, I'm afraid."

Will bowed his head. "Yes, Ma'am. Of course. Whatever the PIB needs."

"Thank you. Hopefully we won't need her, so don't lose any sleep over it."

I turned to look at Will, but he avoided my gaze by staring at the table, where he drew figure eights with his finger. Fine. He wasn't about to let me in. Maybe he never would. I needed someone else to crush on. Being attracted to someone who was never going to return the feelings was a waste of time and emotion. When I got home later, I'd call Liv and see if she wanted to go somewhere for dinner. We could both use a night out.

Angelica got back to the important stuff. "In the meantime, my connection at the police has put out a bulletin for Mrs Valentine and her car. If either one is found, we'll be notified. We'll interview her male friend after we've finished with the art society. We have limited resources, thanks to Drake."

I was about to ask why but then thought better of it. She wouldn't have answered, and I would have felt like an outsider all over again. Once per meeting was enough.

"Any questions?"

Millicent shook her head. "Not from me."

I shook my head.

Will answered, "No, Ma'am."

"Righto. We're done for today. We'll reconvene here tomorrow afternoon at three. You are dismissed."

"Ma'am, just on a personal note. I might go out for dinner with Liv tonight. I'll send you a text if I do."

"Okay, dear. Thanks for letting me know. Enjoy your evening."

"Thanks." I smiled and stood. "See you all later."

Will said, "Bye."

Millicent gave me a little wave and a sad smile. She must still be thinking about Knight. "See you later, Lil."

I waved, conjured my doorway, and stepped through into Angelica's reception room. Ah, it was nice to be home, and what about the commute? If everyone was a witch, there'd be no more peak-hour traffic and less pollution, but more lines for public toilets. But if everyone was a witch, they could make special reception rooms everywhere. That would be cool.

I left the reception room and locked the door behind me. My stomach grumbled. It was two in the afternoon, and I hadn't had lunch. Oh, the horror! As I walked to the kitchen, I felt as if something was missing. I stopped and looked down. My nose tingled as tears moistened my eyes.

Knight.

He'd been with me for just over half a day, but I missed him. He'd been cute and had such strong presence. Maybe I should think about getting a familiar. Would Angelica mind me having an animal inside the house because I couldn't imagine making mine sleep outside? I'd have to have it with me most of the time. And what would I get? A cat, a dog, a fox? Now it was getting complicated. Where did one start when looking for familiars? Were they special animals sold from a witchy store, or could any animal become one? Argh, I so needed to talk to Angelica or Millicent about it. Just another thing to add to my to-do list. At this rate, I'd get through it when I was eighty.

I finally made it into the kitchen where I rustled up grilled cheese and tomato on toast for lunch, after which I called Liv, who agreed to go out for dinner. She said she'd book it and pick me up at seven. Yay. I texted Angelica, then went up for a shower. I only had a few hours to decide what to wear. Would that be enough time? I giggled. Yes, but it was cutting it close. The thought of a night out cheered me up a bit. Who knew? Maybe I'd run into the man of my dreams.

Or maybe not.

CHAPTER 5

I was waiting outside when Olivia turned up at seven on the dot and parked her car in Ma'am's driveway. She hopped out. "Hey, Lily!"

"Hey, yourself. You look gorgeous."

"Oh, these old clothes?" She flopped her hand down in an "it's nothing" gesture. But she really did look gorgeous wearing skintight black jeans, tight white T-shirt, and a black quilted jacket. The outfit looked like it had cost a fortune, especially the jacket.

"Ha ha. Very funny. But you really do look good. You're making it hard for me to find someone. They'll all be staring at you." I grinned. I didn't mind, not really. Well, maybe a little bit. Although, going by who she'd been engaged to, we weren't attracted to the same kind of look.

"What are you worried about? Red is definitely your

colour. I love your shirt. It sets off your blue eyes. They really are stunning."

I was wearing a decent amount of make-up for a change, and yes, I had tried to play up my eyes with black mascara and eyeliner. My eyes were definitely my best feature, and I needed all the help I could get. There was a reason I was twenty-four and still single, and I was beginning to think it was more than my pickiness. Guys didn't approach me often, and at nightclubs, I was always the one left standing around minding my friends' drinks. "Thanks, Liv." I smiled. "So, where are we going?"

"Napoli E. It's Italian, in case the name didn't give it away." She giggled. "The food is awesome, and it has a rather rustic ambiance. It's in the village, actually. We could probably walk." She looked down at my flat boots, and I checked out her footwear—also flat black boots.

"A walk it is. I could use the exercise. I did a lot of sitting today. We had a meeting." I didn't want to mention PIB outside where someone could hear, and now that Olivia was training to be a liaison and researcher for the PIB, she knew what I was talking about.

"Is everything okay?"

"Yes. Well, no. Mrs Valentine's missing." I bit my tongue to stop any lurking tears waiting to embarrass me at the thought of Knight. Tears could be tricky, and they loved to ambush me when I least expected. I knew I needed to toughen up, but it wasn't easy.

Her mouth opened in an O. "Missing?"

"Yes. But let's get going, and I'll fill you in on the way.

Maybe not every detail, because you-know-what confidentiality."

"Not a problem. Let's go."

By the time we'd reached the high street, I'd told her everything I could.

"That's just terrible. Do you think she's still alive?"

I hadn't told her about Knight, just in case that was on a need-to-know basis. I could imagine if word got out, and we were the ones to start the information ball rolling, it might compromise the investigation as whoever had killed him would know we knew.

"I don't know. I hope so, but I have a gut feeling that tells me no."

Olivia looked over her shoulder and smirked. "We have company."

"Huh?" I looked back. Skulking on the other side of the road, wearing jeans and nondescript T-shirts, were two hot men, otherwise known as Beren and Agent Crankypants. "Oh, the poor dears. They've been stuck with protecting-Lily detail."

"Do you think they'd like to join us for dinner?" She looked at them again and smiled. Beren replied with a huge grin.

"Could we maybe just ask Beren? Will was crankier than usual this afternoon. Something to do with work." I still didn't understand it. What could make him not want to work with Dana that badly?

Olivia gently punched me in the upper arm. "Don't be mean. We can't do that."

"Suit yourself." I shrugged and tried to not worry. Chances were they'd say no, since they were on duty.

Olivia waved them over. Beren crossed the road, but Will stayed put, his gaze trained on my face. He was staring at me, causing my core temperature to rise. Argh. He probably hated me right now for ruining what could have been a fun Friday night off-duty. But my stupid body didn't care—it chose to interpret it as the intense stare of an interested man.

Beren reached us. "Good evening, ladies. I understand you're dining out tonight."

"Angelica?" I asked.

"But of course." He smiled.

Oh my God! Olivia had a silly grin. A silly one, not a normal one. One that suggested she might have a thing for Beren. She'd never said anything to me. Maybe she was just enjoying getting back in the game? Beren was a gorgeous man, not to mention really nice and happy. Come to think of it, they'd probably make an awesome couple. Well, there you go. Maybe I should go home and leave them to it? That way, the boys could have a night off. Once I was at Angelica's, I was safe—she had protection wards and an alarm spell on the house that went off if anyone not previously approved entered. Which was quite clever, since I could inadvertently let in someone dangerous if they were posing as a delivery person, for instance.

"Would you guys like to join us for dinner?" Olivia's voice had gone quiet, as if she was afraid to speak but the words were happening regardless.

Beren licked his bottom lip. "We'd ordinarily love to, but we're on duty. Sorry. We do have to keep an eye on you though, and we haven't eaten, so maybe we'll grab a table there by ourselves."

I looked at him like "excuse me," and my eye twitched. "That's so stupid. Why wouldn't you just sit with us?" Not that I really wanted them to because staring across the table at Will all night with his untouchable hotness would be pure torture, but Beren's suggestion really was ridiculous.

"Because you ladies are far too distracting, and we're working." He winked, and Olivia blushed. I suppressed a grin, because they were far too cute.

My stomach gurgled. I would have loved to have stayed and chatted—and watched them make sexy eyes at each other—but I needed to eat. "Well, if that's your final answer, we need to go eat. I'm hungry. Come on, Liv. See you later, B. And thanks again for watching out for me." I smiled at him and grabbed Olivia's hand to drag her towards the restaurant just up the laneway.

Beren waved, and Olivia's resistance soon gave way as she called out, "Bye." Once she was moving in the right direction, I dropped her hand.

"You're no fun, Lily."

"You can hook up with Beren another night, preferably when I'm not there to watch all the googly eyes." I smirked.

Her mouth dropped open. "I was not making googly eyes."

"Yeah, you totally were." I laughed.

"All right. But can you blame me? He's bloody gorgeous."

"No, I can't, and yes, he is. You two would make a really cute couple. You should ask him out."

"Hmm, maybe I will." She smiled. "And here we are, oh hungry one."

The sign for Napoli E hung above the white door of a quaint three-storey orange-brick building, the top storey comprising of dormer windows. Pink and white flowers spilled over planters hanging above each of the white-framed multi-pane ground-floor windows. It was adorable, and I lamented not having my camera with me. I supposed I could have popped it there, but if someone saw, I'd get into a world of trouble with the PIB.

Olivia pushed the door open, and warm, garlic-infused air flowed over us. My mouth watered as I breathed in through my nose, savouring the delicious aroma. My stomach grumbled again.

A short woman with dyed-red hair arranged in a bun intercepted us just inside the door. "Can I help you?"

Olivia smiled. "A table for two, thanks, booked in the name of Olivia."

The woman went to a nearby table and checked out her booking book. Did it have a technical name? I mean, booking book was awkward, and I was sure people working in restaurants didn't call it that. Damn it! I had to know.

The woman grabbed two menus. "Please follow me."

The main restaurant area was full of timber: timber floors, rolled timber panelling a third of the way up the walls, and a similar light-yellowy-orange timber for tables and chairs. Yikes, it was like being in a sauna in the seventies, minus the steam and eucalyptus smell, but the place was over three-quarters full already, so the food must be good.

We took our seats, and she handed us menus.

I couldn't help myself—I just had to know. "Excuse me?"

She smiled. "Yes?"

"What do you call that book you write down bookings in?"

She blinked, probably wondering why the stupid question, and I didn't blame her. "That's the reservations book."

I blushed. I was so stupid. Of course it was. My brain totally sucked sometimes. "Thanks."

"No problem." Her bemused expression did nothing to contain my embarrassment. "Can I get you ladies a drink?"

Ooh, a drink would be nice. I needed to relax after the day I'd had, and I hadn't had a proper drink since that night at the wine bar with Olivia and her deceased fiancé, Frederick. "Do you have Baileys?"

"We certainly do."

"Can I grab a double on the rocks?"

She tapped her electronic device with a little pen thing, then looked at Olivia. "And for you?"

"I'll have a bourbon and Coke, thanks."

The woman left, and I turned to Olivia, who was seated opposite me on our two-person table. "So, when are you coming to live with us?" I didn't want to seem too needy, so

I left out the fact that because Angelica was always working, I was often by myself. Not that I didn't like my own space, but even I had my limits and needed company sometimes, especially with the drama factory my life had become since I'd arrived here.

She grinned. "I meant to tell you. I had a chat with my parents, and they've agreed I'm doing okay, so they're fine with me moving, not that it's that far away from where they are. I'm planning on moving my stuff next weekend."

I clapped excitedly. "Yay! Well, now we have something to celebrate." Our drinks arrived, and I held mine up. "To some fun times at Angelica's."

"Cheers." Olivia clinked her glass against mine.

We ordered—me, linguini marinara and Olivia, pizza. Dinner arrived, and we ate, but in the middle of the meal, a sharp pain lanced through my middle. "Ow!" I dropped my fork and pressed my hand against my stomach.

Olivia placed her knife and fork on the table. "Are you okay?"

I stayed still for a moment, to check. "Yeah. I think—" Another spasm of pain mangled my stomach. I clutched my middle and gritted my teeth. Then, through excruciating cramps, the tingle of power on the back of my neck registered.

I tried to breathe through the agony and looked up. Across the room, his face shadowed by a baseball cap, was a beefy, broad-shouldered man. The ambient lighting made it hard to clearly see his features, but he was familiar, and he was staring at me.

He narrowed his eyes and nodded, then brought his finger to his throat and made a cutting motion across his neck. The pain subsided long enough for me to raise my brows. Now I was being threatened with a cliché? If that man wasn't a witch, I'd laugh, but he was, and he wanted me dead. But why?

Then two things slammed into me at once. The first was another breath-stealing cramp, and the other—well, I knew who he was, and yep, he totally wanted me dead. I'd killed his friend in that car crash in Paris.

He was working for the enemy.

My eyes watered, and I struggled to get the words out. "Olivia, you have to pay the bill and then go and get the guys. I'm being tortured. Tell them I'll meet them at Angelica's."

She wrinkled her brow, maybe wondering if I was joking. Even I knew this was not normal dinner conversation.

"Nope. Not joking. I can't run, but I'm going to stagger to the bathroom and go home via the toilet. I can't make a doorway here, and if we leave, that guy will be onto me before the guys can intervene. So I'll get up first; then you can do what you have to. Oh, and please take my bag. Is that okay?"

She nodded, her eyes huge with concern. "Are you sure you'll be all right?"

"Yes," I gritted out while struggling to stand. I supported myself with one hand on the table. The other hand clutched my midsection. I pushed off the table and hurried to the toilets, my steps tiny but speedy. I imagined I looked like a penguin taking a runoff before diving into the water, which was far better than imagining what the hell was happening to my insides. Was it possible for a witch to magic a knife inside a person?

Just as I reached the toilet door, I turned my head. Beefy thug had followed me, which was no surprise. Another few metres, and he'd have me. His gravelly, heavily accented voice cut through my pain. "You killed my brother. Now, I kill you." As he approached, he raised his fist and jerked it one hundred and eighty degrees, similar to the motion of turning a car key in the ignition sans fingers. My tormented stomach felt as if someone had applied clamps and was twisting my insides together until they were squished pulp. Breath wouldn't come, and tears tore down my face unbidden.

But as much as my body wanted to, I was not going to fall to my knees and give up. I shoved the door open, fell through into the bathroom, and mumbled the travelling spell whilst picturing the coordinates to Angelica's reception room. The toilet door slammed closed behind me.

My portal appeared, thank God, because in the state I was in, I could have made a mistake. I stumbled through, narrowly avoiding touching the edges and amputating something. Landing on hands and knees in Angelica's reception room, I could fully appreciate the prettiness of her circular blue-and-white rug. The pain had retreated to an ache, but whatever he'd done had wrung me dry. I collapsed the rest of the way to the floor and curled into a ball.

The door burst open, then Angelica was on the floor, her hand on my shoulder. "Oh my goodness. Lily, what happened? Are you hurt?"

I relaxed somewhat and gingerly sat up, expecting another shock of agony to rip through me. My face radiated heat, and I lifted a hand to feel my brow. Damp clamminess was the best way to describe how that felt. Ew. The whole experience had been similar to surviving near-fatal gastro. "I'm not sure. That other guy from the van, you know, the ones who were after me, showed up at the restaurant. He did something with magic and tortured me. I don't know if there's any damage, but my innards have been through the wringer."

"Let's get you moved. I would imagine the boys aren't too far behind you." She grabbed my arm and helped me stand.

We headed into the hallway. I was still waddling—penguin steps were all I could manage right now. Just as we reached the living room, footsteps thudded behind us. I hadn't even made it to the Chesterfields when Beren said, "Lily! Are you all right? Let me have a look."

I stopped, and he edged around me. Angelica released my arm as Beren grabbed the other one, then placed one palm on my stomach. His brow furrowed, and his gaze intently held mine, worry radiating from him. "Olivia told me what happened. Let me see if he did any damage."

"We got here as fast as we could." Olivia stepped around me and stood next to Beren. Her eyes were wide, face pale.

"Thanks, Liv. You did good." I tried to give her a smile, but it probably came out looking like a grimace.

"Okay, let's get this done." Beren shut his eyes. Warmth spread through the ache. A spasm caused me to flinch, but then all the discomfort faded away, leaving me tender but, I assumed, healed.

Beren opened his eyes. "Done. You'll be fine, but it could have been much worse. It looks like he used his power to squeeze your stomach and intestines. If it had lasted much longer, the lack of blood supply or burst blood vessels could have done some serious damage. And if that had happened, you may not have gotten help in time. Everything was bruised, and there were two small bleeds, but I've healed it all."

I wrapped my arms around him and buried my head in his chest. "Thank you so much, B." I released him and stepped back.

"Any time." He grinned.

"Come and sit down, everyone, and I'll make some tea," Angelica said from her spot on one of the Chesterfields.

I sat next to her, Beren and Olivia sitting on the other lounge. Someone was noticeably absent. Did he care that little? "Where's William?" I asked, trying not to sound like it mattered.

His voice came from the hallway, and the rest of him soon followed. "Here I am. Sorry I'm late. I had a criminal to chase. Unfortunately, he got away." He strode to the Chesterfields and made me scoot over so he could sit next to me. He took my hand and looked into my eyes. "I'm so sorry, Lily."

The good old butterflies everyone loved took flight in my stomach. Honestly, my stomach had been through enough for one night. "That's okay. You tried. He's really pissed at me for killing his brother."

"Ah, so that's who he is. But don't worry, Lily; we'll catch him." William squeezed my hand, then didn't release it. Hmm, interesting and so very nice. His hand was warm and comforting and sent tingles through my body, and as much as I'd tried not to over the last few weeks, I'd daydreamed about holding his hand many times, if not doing a lot more, but it was best not get into that.

William continued. "Beren, did you get his magic signature when you checked out Lily?"

"I had to heal her, Will. That bastard did some damage." He shook his head, and a muscle in his jaw bulged. "But yes, I got it. When we've finished here, we'll go into the Bureau and check it out, add it to the database if it's not there."

Will nodded. "Good. I imagine if he were being paid to kidnap her, whoever hired him wouldn't be too pleased at his attempt to kill her. I'd say he's gone rogue."

I swallowed. Just freaking great. "So, does that mean there'll be new people sent to snatch me, *and* I have to worry about this jerk-face?"

"I'm afraid so. Just trust that Beren and I will do everything we can to protect you. But it also means no more going out unless we've cleared it first."

My eyes widened. Nooooo! I already had people following me 24/7—now I was going to be practically housebound again? I pursed my lips, the butterflies in my stomach morphing into stinging wasps that fuelled my anger one tiny jab at a time. I snatched my hand out of William's.

Angelica placed a gentle hand on my thigh. "I'm sorry, dear, but he's right. At least until we've caught this man. If William hadn't suggested it, I would have."

Olivia smiled. "I know this doesn't solve your problem, Lily, but why don't I move in tomorrow? That way you'll have company. Once I'm settled in, we can watch a movie tomorrow night and get takeout."

I grinned, and just like that, things were so much better. "I'd like that. Thank you, Liv. Are you sure you're ready?" I knew she'd had a tough time since my brother had killed her thieving, cheating fiancé, and her parents had been the rocks she'd needed them to be. I didn't want her to do anything before she was ready, and moving out of their house was a big step for her at this point.

"Well, I was going to move next weekend anyway." She shrugged. "I'm ready. In fact, I'm really looking forward to it." Her grin said she told the truth.

"Well, that's settled then." Angelica smiled and stood. "It's time for William and Beren to get back to headquarters. Because of what's transpired tonight, I'll stay here. I've checked all the wards, and the house is secure, but I'll feel better if I'm here, and I can keep an eye on things." She turned her gaze on Olivia. "Are you all right to drive home, dear? In fact, I'll send Beren with you. He can pop into headquarters when you're home safely."

Olivia turned to Beren, her smile shy. "Are you sure it's no trouble?"

He grinned. "Since when is escorting a beautiful woman home trouble?" He winked and held out his arm for her to take.

She laughed and linked her arm through his. "Well, since you put like that, how can I refuse?"

I grinned in spite of all the drama of the past hour. At least one night could have a happy ending for someone, and hey, William had held my hand. I looked at him. "Thanks, Will. Sorry for getting upset. It's just—"

"Hey, it's okay. I understand. Just stay safe." He tapped my nose with a finger. "See you later." How could such an innocent tap to the nose have my heart racing like that?

He said his goodbyes to everyone else, then popped away. Beren and Olivia left via the front door, both giving me a hug. I stood in the doorway, next to Angelica, and waved as Olivia's car backed down the driveway. Then I turned and went inside. Angelica shut and locked the door, then followed me to the bottom of the stairs.

"Are you heading to bed, dear?"

"Yeah. I'm exhausted. I'm going to have a shower first though. I feel violated. Even though he didn't touch me, his magic was inside me." I shuddered and wished I could open my stomach and wash inside there too.

"If you need to talk, let me know."

"Thanks. I will." I made my way up the two flights of

stairs, hoping sleep would find me tonight. But after the day I'd had, I highly doubted it. And my doubt was well founded.

Later, tucked up safely in bed, there was no escape. When I closed my eyes, my attacker stared back at me.

And there went sleep, riding into the darkness on horse-back, my hopes sitting behind her, arms clinging to her waist, head thrown back in glee. I could hear her laughter from here.

Universe: 5243, Lily: 0.

I was totally out of my league.

CHAPTER 6

After drifting off to sleep sometime after 3:00 a.m., I woke at nine to a knock on my door. "Come in."

Angelica poked her face in my room. "Olivia just called. She'll be here with her things shortly. It would be nice if you were downstairs to greet her."

"Thanks for waking me. I feel like I've been thrown off a cliff and hit every boulder on the way down." I sat up and stretched my stiff neck to one side, then the other, and yawned.

"You do look tired, dear. Maybe have an afternoon nap."

I yawned again. "Yep. I think I'll have to."

"I'll leave you to it, but don't be long." She shut the door, and I got dressed, went to the toilet, brushed my teeth, and then headed downstairs. I'd had just enough time to guzzle a coffee when the doorbell rang.

Olivia! I hurried to the front door, but Angelica had beaten me to it. Olivia stood there, a green lamp in hand and her parents behind her. Her father was carrying an antique timber chair, and her mother held a doona.

"Welcome! Please, come in. I'm Angelica DuPree. Pleased to meet you."

Olivia stood to the side and said, "This is my mother, Cassandra, and my dad, Robert."

Angelica shook both of their hands in turn, then ushered them inside. "Lily, please show them where Olivia's room is. She can have the one next to yours."

I grinned and started up the stairs. I should really be carrying something, so I motioned Olivia past me—she knew where the room was, as she'd visited a few times and seen my room—then waited for her dad to pass before I took the doona from her mother. "Here, let me carry that."

"It's no trouble, Lily."

"I know. But I want to help." She let go, and I commandeered the bedding and took it to Olivia's new room.

Upon inspection, her parents were happy, and we all went down to grab more things, although there wasn't that much more. Two suitcases, a couple of throw pillows, her normal pillow, some sheets, a box of books, a small flat-screen TV, and laptop.

Her parents stayed for a cup of tea—so English—then they hugged her goodbye and left. Angelica went out to the garden, leaving Olivia and me to ourselves. "So, what do you want to do?" I asked.

"What about we start our movie marathon early? We can watch on my TV."

"Sounds awesome to me. Let's do this."

We spent the day watching chick flicks and munching on chocolate Olivia had brought. One of the films was my favourite—*Bridesmaids*—and another came a close second, *Spy*, starring Melissa McCarthy. I loved her. She seemed as if she really had her shit together. I wanted to be her when I grew up. We also managed to fit in *Miss Congeniality*. Ah, Sandra Bullock, another of my faves. The company and entertainment managed to force away thoughts of Knight, Mrs Valentine, and the evil bastard who'd tried to kill me.

By early evening, the three of us sat around the kitchen table, finishing a dinner of Indian takeout, when Angelica's mobile rang. She answered and had a short conversation with Will. She hung up. "Have you had enough, ladies?"

"Yes, thanks. That was yum." I smiled.

Olivia nodded. "Yes. I'm so full I'm about to burst."

"Good. Time to pack up and get moving." She swept her hand across the table, and everything disappeared. Olivia started. I'd forgotten she wasn't used to seeing magic every five minutes. But then again, neither was I. No matter how often I'd witnessed it, sometimes it managed to take me by surprise.

I smirked. "You'll get used to it… eventually."

"That was awesome!"

Angelica smiled, looking rather proud. "Olivia, I hope you don't mind, but I'm taking Lily to a meeting at the

Bureau, but since you're not working for us yet, I'll have to leave you here."

"That's fine. I have studying to do anyway. I'll see you when you get back."

Oh, no. Another meeting. I hated going to the Bureau, but maybe there'd been a breakthrough on Mrs Valentine's case. Then I remembered: William and that agent he was unhappy about were supposed to have done some interviews this afternoon. Hopefully they'd found something.

I made my doorway to the Bureau's reception room and stepped through. Angelica seemed to be on call twenty-four hours a day. What a tedious thing to sign up for. When could you ever really relax? You'd be on tenterhooks all the time, anticipating a call.

Ma'am, which is how I thought of her whenever I was at the Bureau, and even sometimes at home when she was being particularly bossy, walked slightly ahead of me and opened the boardroom door. She went straight to the seat at the head of the table and sat. James sat on her left, Millicent to her right. Phew, that meant Drake wasn't here. Score! My happiness was short-lived, however, when I spied the stunning black-haired woman sitting next to Will. And her hair wasn't just black; it was straight and glossy, falling past her shoulders to rest just above her perky boobs. How did I know they were perky? They were buoyant in a push-up bra, floating in a sea of creamy flesh. The smooth mounds were pushed into cleavage that was prominently displayed in the gap of her white PIB shirt. She'd dispensed with the tie and had the first three shirt buttons undone.

Her boobs weren't the worst of it, however. She leaned towards Will with a sultry smirk on her face, as if she owned him. And who knew? Maybe she did. Then my thoughts careened to an unexpected halt as they smashed head-on into a wall of oh-my-God-she-must-be-his-ex.

I sat opposite her, next to Beren, and tried not to stare with a horrified look on my face, but I couldn't help it; I swear. Her grin told me she understood but didn't care. She fixed her brown eyes on me and smiled. It wasn't the warm smile of a soon-to-be friend but the satisfied grin of a shark before it eats dinner. I had a new appreciation for lower-food-chain creatures.

Millicent's sympathetic gaze confirmed the worst. My cheeks heated. I was such an idiot. Why did I have to be attracted to him? No wonder they called it a crush—because unrequited feelings had a way of grinding your heart to a pulp. And my chest really did hurt.

I swallowed and looked at William. He avoided my gaze, finding something on the empty table much more interesting. Coward.

Angelica cleared her throat. "Lily, I'd like you to meet one of the team. Agent Dana Lam is one of our best. She's been working in our New York office, and we're glad to have her back." Why was Ma'am torturing me? Could she not see what everyone else was apparently cognizant of? Had I forgotten to clean my messes one too many times? I'd hate to see what she did to people who seriously pissed her off. Ma'am smiled towards the woman. "Dana conducted the interviews with Agent Blakesley this afternoon."

I took a deep breath and smiled, ignoring the fact that I wanted to cry. Will wasn't mine and never had been. "Lovely to meet you, Agent Lam. I hope you guys got some useful information today." Oops, I hadn't meant for that to come out snarky. Was it snarky?

"The information I get is always useful." Okay, so it was a touch snarky. Dana leaned even closer to Will, laying her hand on his arm. "I'll let my better half... ah, Will, explain." She tittered as if she'd accidentally been too familiar about him. Yeah, we totally believed her, not. But I did agree: he was better than her.

He gave her a narrow-eyed stare, and she removed her hand. Hmm, maybe things weren't that great between them, which made sense if she was the one who broke his heart beyond repair.

Will straightened his already-straight tie, then spoke. "We interviewed three of the five board members. Two are away until tomorrow and have supposedly been away for the last week, but we're yet to check it out. We'll get that information tomorrow when we interview them."

Ma'am lifted her arm, and a bunch of paper appeared in her hand. She kept one stapled lot and passed the rest to James, who slid it along the table to Millicent. Eventually the pile of papers reached Will. He took one handout and passed the rest across the table. I took a copy and gave the last one to Beren.

Ma'am said, "These are the transcripts of the interviews. Please read them tonight."

Gee, there must be thirty pages here. How did they get

them typed so quickly? Oh, that's right: witches didn't have to type. Looked as if I'd have lots of bedtime reading tonight. "Have we found out any more about her will?" I wasn't an expert at these things, but money was always a good motivator for murderers, especially in TV shows and books.

Ma'am shook her head. "I'm afraid not. We want to at least confirm she's missing by talking to everyone who knows her before we insist on legal documents from her lawyer. As you know, this isn't a fully fledged investigation until we have a body or confirmation of Mrs Valentine's disappearance. The PIB has *costs* to consider." Her poker face dropped, and she did one full eye-roll. It was expertly executed, and if I didn't know better, I'd say she'd done plenty in her time.

"Has anyone interviewed her boyfriend, Henry?" I didn't think he'd done anything, but maybe he knew if she had any enemies, although why anyone would have something against her was beyond me.

Millicent spoke. "I was going to call him tomorrow; his details are in Mrs Valentine's phone. I was hoping you'd come with me, make it less scary for him, since you've met him before. From what we can tell, he never stood to gain from her will, and unless they weren't getting along, he probably has no motive, but he may be worried because we have to ask him certain sensitive questions. It will be a good opportunity for you to learn something about our procedures, too, Lily."

"Ah, okay. That sounds good." At least it would be better

than sitting at home, and maybe he had some useful information.

James leaned towards Ma'am and whispered something. She nodded, and he stood. "I've another meeting to get to. Sorry I can't help you out today, Will, but I'm hoping to be free of this other case soon."

"Not a problem." Will's frown said it most likely was a problem, but he could deal.

"Good luck, team," James said, then stepped into his doorway and disappeared. Drake must really be trying to make things difficult for Ma'am.

Beren, who had been so quiet for the whole meeting that I'd forgotten he was there, said, "When will we get the autopsy report for the fox?"

"Tomorrow afternoon, at this stage. Unless anything untoward happens, we'll meet back here at six tomorrow evening. Any questions?" She stood in the silence. "Good. Team, you're dismissed."

Beren turned to me. "How are you feeling today?"

Were we talking emotionally or physically? I'd give him the easy answer. "Great, thanks. Other than being tired, I'm fine. You really are good at what you do. I was wondering how the guy was able to do that to me."

Beren hesitated before answering, "I can do it too, and so can Will, to a certain extent. I'm better at it than him because healing is my other skill. Usually, skills come in pairs of polar opposites. If you can heal, you can hurt, but I have no idea how he managed to attack you without touching you. I mean, it can be done, but only from very close. The fact that he could do it from across the room is worrying."

"Gee, thanks. I feel so much better now." I gently punched his arm.

"Happy to help." He winked. "But seriously, it's best you know as much as possible. I have to get going, but tonight, ask Ma'am to teach you a blocking or return-to-sender spell. They pretty much do what they say."

"Why hasn't anyone taught them to me yet? They sound kind of essential, especially since I've had a bloody target on my back since I got here."

"Because, dear, they take more magic than you're used to using. Your spell needs to repel someone else's magic, so it can be as taxing as a physical fight, especially if you haven't built up your magic strength." Angelica stood next to Beren's chair, handbag on her shoulder, ready to leave. "But Beren is right. Your life will be easier if you can protect yourself to some degree. We'll work on it sometime in the next few days. Now, if you'll excuse me, I must go." She didn't even step; she just disappeared.

"How did she do that?"

Dana answered, "She's extremely good at what she does, so good that she can make a doorway around herself. But don't worry, darling. I'm sure you'll be able to travel by yourself one day. Never like Angelica or I, but still, something is better than nothing."

Before I could answer, she grabbed Will's hand, and they both disappeared. I turned to Beren, my mouth hanging open. What a b—

Beren put his hand on my shoulder. "Don't worry, Lily. She likes to rile people up. Don't let her get to you."

Easy for him to say. I bet she'd never insulted him, then run away before he could defend himself. And I bet they'd never been competing for the same person's affection. Argh, was I pathetic or what? I didn't do competing for a man. If he didn't want me, well, that was that. Pushing the issue was way too desperate and beneath me.

"Beren's right." Millicent was still sitting at the other end of the table. "She was never very nice, but she is a good agent, although William could never see the bad side of her until it was too late. I have faith he won't make the same mistake twice. Anyway,"—she quickly covered her mouth as she yawned—"I'm tired. Time to go home. I'll pick you up at ten tomorrow morning. Is that okay?"

"Yep. Ten's fine. Should I wear the PIB threads?"

"Yes, that would be good. See you tomorrow. Night." She pushed her chair back and stood, then took a step to the right. Gone.

Beren and I said our goodbyes, and within a few seconds, I was back in Ma'am's reception room. I raced up to Olivia's room and knocked on her door.

"Come in."

I opened the door and went in. I couldn't help my cheesy grin. It was nice to have company my own age. "How's the studying going?"

She closed her laptop and turned. "Good, thanks. Getting there. How was the meeting?"

"Meh, the usual."

"That great huh?" She laughed.

I sat on her bed and debated whether I should tell her or not. Self-pity won in the end. "I met Will's ex-girlfriend. She's an agent, one of their *best*, apparently. She's also one of their rudest, cattiest, b—"

"Oh no! I'm sorry, Lily. I know you've never admitted to much, but we can all tell you have it bad for him."

"And you admitting I've been making a fool out of myself for weeks and weeks is supposed to make me feel better how?"

She sat next to me. "Just that you can talk about it with me, and probably Millicent for that matter. I don't suppose you'd want to talk to your brother about liking his friend."

I snorted. "You suppose right." I took a deep breath, then sighed. "Anyway, that's it. Can we talk about something else?"

"Yeah, sure."

True to her word, we chatted about everything else but the Will situation until we were both yawning—it had been a big day for both of us. We said goodnight, and I showered and went to bed.

And just for a change, sleep came swiftly. Looked as if heartache was good for something.

CHAPTER 7

The next morning, I woke up early and read over the information Angelica had given us last night. All the interviewees were sad she was missing but hopeful she'd turn up. Had anyone fought with her recently? No. Was the society desperate to get their hands on the money she had willed them? Supposedly not. And from how they spoke of Mrs Valentine, they all adored her and her artwork. So it didn't look as if those board members were good candidates for kidnapping or murder, at least not of Mrs Valentine.

Millicent arrived at ten on the dot. The morning was chilly and raining. What kind of summer was this? I guessed the English kind. The route Millicent took was familiar, and I was surprised when she pulled into Mrs Valentine's driveway.

"Why are we here? Does he live with her?"

"No. He's just checking on the place, and he does her bookwork for the art classes. He said since he was going to be here anyway, that we should come here."

"Fair enough."

I was dressed in the PIB uniform, but I didn't have my camera, which made me feel awkward. My Nikon gave me something to hold, kind of like a security blanket. I patted my hips, then around the front of my trousers. Ooh, pockets! My hands went straight in, and I almost sighed with happiness. Crisis averted.

Henry opened the barn door, and joy of joys, he was dressed. My no-camera awkwardness would have been nothing compared to my oh-my-God-he's-naked awkwardness. It probably would've thrown Millicent as well.

"Good morning, ladies."

"Good morning, Mr Murphy. I'm Agent Millicent Bianchi. Thank you for seeing us on such short notice."

"It's the least I can do." He stepped aside, and we walked in. "Haven't I seen you somewhere before?" he asked me.

"Yes. I'm Lily Bianchi. I've taken a couple of Mrs Valentine's life-drawing classes."

He smiled. "That's right! Oh, you were here the last afternoon we saw her, weren't you?" His smile fell, and he shut the door.

"Yes. So, you haven't heard from her since then?"

"She called me that night, after the argument with her brother. She was going for a drive to blow off steam." His shoulders dropped. "That was the last time I spoke to her. We've never gone this long without speaking. Something bad's definitely happened."

Millicent cocked her head to the side. "I'm so sorry, Mr Murphy. Would you rather we sat down while we had this conversation?"

He nodded, a forlorn expression on his face, and led us to the three-seat couch at the other end of the room. My eyes widened. Oh no. It was the sex couch. And there weren't any other chairs close by. There was an armchair, but it was about five metres from the couch. Could I get away with sitting at a distance?

Millicent must have seen the photo—I'd given the memory card to Angelica—because when Henry sat, she hesitated and looked around. I smirked. She was totally looking for an out, as I had. Was it going to be a race for the far-away chair?

"Please sit," Henry said.

She had no choice but to gingerly sit next to him, although she made sure to perch right on the edge of the cushion. "Hurry up, Lily." She patted the spot next to her, ensuring I had no escape. I raised my brow but then mimicked her when I sat. These pants were going straight in the wash when I got home.

"So, what would you like to know?" He looked at Millicent.

Millicent pulled a notebook and pen out of her bag. "When was the last time you saw Mrs Valentine?"

"Thursday, at life drawing. I was the subject. That was

when she got the phone call and left. Knight went with her, and I haven't seen either of them since. I have a bad feeling, but I know Knight would protect her with his life."

My shoulders sagged. This wasn't promising.

Millicent scribbled notes, then asked another question. "I'm sorry to have to ask this, Mr. Murphy, but had you and Mrs Valentine had any disagreements lately that might make her leave for a while?"

He furrowed his brow. "Of course not! We had the perfect relationship. She got me, and I got her. Our love of art has been a source of much joy between us, and if you knew her, you would know it's impossible to fight with her. She's such a bubbly, giving soul." He shook his head. "I would never hurt her." His eyes shone. Were those tears?

He seemed sincere enough, but James's truth-seeing ability would have been good here, just to be sure.

"Is it okay if I ask something?"

Millicent nodded. "Of course, Miss Bianchi. Go ahead."

"When you didn't hear from Mrs Valentine, why didn't you contact the police?" I felt like a mean witch asking that, but someone had to. It was a pertinent question.

"I figured she was just somewhere blowing off steam, you know, after the big row with her brother. She's done that before, gone off to cool down for a couple of days."

"After you two fought?" Was it going to be that easy to trip him up? Millicent gave me a nod, probably indicating I'd asked a good question.

"Well, yes. There was that one time, about a year ago. I

never said we'd never fought, just that it was unusual and not recently. The last time she took off was about a month ago, after she'd had a run-in with one of the other entrants in an art competition. She was right mad, she was. Didn't see her for three days. She finally came home, her old happy self."

Millicent made more notes, then looked up. "And who was this woman, and do you know what they fought about?"

He sneered. "Maddison Archer. You could almost call her Ida's nemesis." His laugh was bitter. "Those two could barely be civil around each other, although it was always Maddison's fault. She was jealous of how good Ida's paintings were. Ida always won the local art prizes here, and even some in London. Maddison always accused my Ida of cheating, although how you can cheat at painting is beyond me."

Now we were getting somewhere. But was jealousy over an art prize reason enough to kill? I guessed if entering art competitions was your whole life and you always lost to the same person, it could get irritating.

Millicent stopped writing and looked at Henry. "Where did she go last time she needed some space?"

"Brighton. She loves it down there, she does. She always says it feeds her artistic soul. It's the sea air and the gulls, apparently."

"Any hotel or house in particular?" Millicent used a soothing tone, which I supposed was because he wasn't really a suspect. How must he feel, his girlfriend missing and other people thinking he'd done it? Unfortunately, it was often the male partner, but Henry seemed so gentle that I found it hard to believe he'd hurt her, plus he didn't have a motive. At least none that we knew.

"Not that I know of. I'm sorry I can't help you more. I've called all her friends, but none of them have heard from her. I just don't know what I'll do if anything has happened to her." He shook his head and clasped his hands together in his lap. "I'm thinking of taking the train down to Brighton, see if I can find her."

Millicent closed her notebook. "Did you return to her house at all that night?"

His eyes widened. I wasn't sure if he was offended by her question, which implied we didn't trust him, or he was surprised we suspected him of being there. How he answered would tell us whether he deserved our trust.

"I was returning her keys. I had to lock up for her that afternoon—she left before the end of the class. I promised I'd bring them back."

Wow, did we look like meanies.

Millicent nodded. "Did anything seem unusual?"

He shook his head. "No. It was dark. I let myself in, left her keys on the hook beside the front door, then left."

Millicent put her notebook and pen in her bag. "If you remember anything else or hear from her or any of her friends, please let us know." She pulled a card out of her bag. "Here's my card. Don't hesitate to get in touch if you think of anything else that might help."

He nodded. "Thank you. I'll be sure to."

We stood, and he showed us out. We hurried to the car through the rain. I jumped in and hugged myself to get warm. Millicent got in and started the engine. Ah, blessed heat. I held my palms in front of the air vents, which were blowing hot air, and looked up at Mrs Valentine's house.

Melancholy wove itself around me, and I sighed.

Millicent's voice was soft. "Are you thinking about Knight?"

"Yeah. We failed him. Poor fox. I miss him too, which is crazy, since I hardly spent any time with him, but he was so cute, and I've never met an animal that I could actually talk to before. And he was sad about his witch disappearing. He knew things that could've helped us find out what's going on. I just know it. He'd be upset to know what had happened."

"I know." She sighed too, then took a deep breath and blew it out loudly. "Time to go. We're going to have to figure this out without Knight's help. Maybe he's watching down from somewhere, thankful we're on the case." She smiled.

"I hope so. Where to now?"

"I'd like to duck into headquarters and speak to Ma'am. We'll need to interview that Maddy woman—well, at least Will needs to."

"And *Dana*. Don't forget her." I folded my arms, cranky. She was such a smug witch and mean, not to mention I hated myself for letting her get to me. I needed to get over Will ASAP. This infatuation wasn't healthy. It was making me unhappy more than happy, and that was a good sign to drop it. And yeah, I knew it wouldn't be easy, but I'd have to decide there was no chance of us getting together and stop hoping.

"Yes, Dana."

"Well, don't you have any sister-in-lawry advice? I could use some right about now."

She gave me a side-eyes glance and smirked. "So, you're ready to admit to liking Will, are you?"

I rolled my eyes. "Yeah, yeah. I think he's hot, okay. I've been attracted to him since the moment I met him, but he was cranky." I laughed. "And when I found out who he was, I didn't think dating one of James's best friends was a good idea."

"You know James wouldn't care. I mean, he would care, but he knows Will's a good guy. He already trusts your welfare to him and Beren. I honestly don't think there'd be a problem if you dated either of them. Just don't date one, then the other." She snorted.

My mouth dropped open. "You can't be serious!"

"He he, no. But if you like Will, just go for it."

Wow, really? Now she tells me. I guess that's what happened when you kept your feelings to yourself and didn't open up to people. I couldn't help thinking it was all a little too late. "But what about when it all goes to hell? Get-togethers would be awkward."

"Possibly. Let me tell you something about Will. He doesn't commit easily, and when he does, he takes even longer to let go. He's the type of guy who isn't afraid to work for a relationship, and he's loyal. Once he's in, he's all in. That pretty much goes for everything he does." She put her blinker on and turned down my street.

"Well, thanks for the info, but he's not interested. I just have to figure out how to get over my crush."

"What?" She shook her head. "Lily, he likes you. I can tell. James and I have even had a conversation about it." She grinned. "All the things he's done—waiting for you in the hospital after the crash, taking you for coffee in Paris—and he's even spoken to James about you a couple of times."

If I were a dog and her message was the crinkling of food packaging, my ears would have pricked up. I sat up straight and turned to her instead, as she pulled into Angelica's driveway. I wanted to beat my head against the window for asking, but I couldn't help it. "What did he say?"

She turned the car off and looked at me. "Not much. You know Will. But he offered to watch you as often as James wanted, and he said he liked you, although not in any specific context. But we can tell. Plus, he kind of skirted around the subject of whether James would be upset if he asked you out."

I swallowed. This was good news, right? But that was then, and this was now, plus he never bothered to follow up, so maybe he wasn't super serious, or James and Millicent were reading too much into it, à la me. "Well, that's all in the past. Dana's here, and she wants her man back. Why did they break up anyway?"

She sighed, then frowned. "Yeah, Dana does want him back. I suppose you'll just have to take a step back and see what happens. But she's no good for him. When she got the job offer in New York, they were still together, but after a couple of weeks, she started cheating on him. They'd been together for three years." She paused and stared at me, likely assessing how I was taking the information. She bit her lip, and my stomach took a dive, but in a bad way.

"What, Mill? Just spill. Do they have kids together or something?" I didn't want to know, but I did. As everyone knew, I was a Band-Aid ripper offer.

"No, nothing like that, but they were engaged."

My heart stopped, or maybe that was just the pause between beats. Okay, so I was being overly dramatic, but what else was new? That was it. She'd won. She'd hurt him, but if she realised her mistake and he wanted to give it another go, who was I to get in the way? It wasn't as if we'd even been on one date. They had history—messy and painful, but it was a shared life, something I couldn't compete with.

I shrugged and pretended a hole of gargantuan proportions hadn't just opened inside me and sucked all my emotions out. Besides, I'd been through much worse. Remembering that I'd lost my parents was always such a great reality check. I'd get over this and move on. "It's okay, Mill. I won't pretend I'm not sad about it, but what can you do? It is what it is, and I'm fine." I turned to her and smiled. "Come on. Let's go inside, and you can travel from there."

She grabbed my forearm as I leaned to get out of the car. "Don't give up yet. I mean, maybe don't get your hopes all the way up, but I'm pretty sure he's done with her, at least in a romantic way. If you're meant to be together, it'll happen, right?"

"Yep. And in the meantime, I've got a lot of stuff to do, including finding Mrs Valentine. Come on." I slipped out of her grasp and went inside.

CHAPTER 8

That afternoon, after having lunch with Olivia, who was going to get more studying done, I went to the local art gallery that was run by the West-erham Art Society to see if I could find any clues as to Mrs Valentine's whereabouts. I'd okayed it with Ma'am, who was reluctant, but since we now knew my attacker's magic signature, Ma'am had put a detection spell on me. If he came within one hundred metres of me, an alarm would sound in my head and Ma'am's. It would likely be annoying for her, but if she was happy to do it that way, I was happy. If the alarm went off, I was to get myself to a private space and travel home straight away.

Millicent was desk-bound for the afternoon, and Beren and William were busy, so I had two other agents tailing me from a distance. Johnson was a well-built, six-foot-four black-skinned man, and Smith was a petite, wiry olive-skinned woman who was shorter than me, but her stance said not to mess with her. And I wasn't going to. I did feel safe with them watching out for me, and I gave them a small wave just before I went into the gallery, which was a ten-minute walk from home.

A white converted two-storey brick cottage held the Westerham Art Society and Gallery. It was a few minutes' walk north of the high street, near the Westerham Hall. As usual, there was no street parking, which didn't bother me, because, of course, I didn't have a car. I hoped the agents didn't mind walking in the rain. I'd gotten a snazzy yellow raincoat and purple gumboots, and I wore them now, wanting to look as normal as possible. I was undercover. Angelica had never said I was, but that's how I was playing this. It was exciting being sneaky, and believing I was under-cover made me feel more important, even if it was only in my head. I think Angelica was just humouring me in letting me come here, but who knew? I might find information because people didn't have their guards up around me, and since I wasn't an actual PIB employee, I could get away with it, technically.

When I entered, a bell tinkled above the door. Cute. I'd brought my knapsack, which held my wallet, phone, camera, and a bottle of water. I wasn't sure if I'd be allowed to use the camera to shoot the paintings, but I wanted to be prepared.

The room's dark blue carpet and stark white walls were a dramatic backdrop for the myriad of varying-sized paint-ings hanging in there. "Can I help you?" A man in jeans, blue plaid shirt, and camel-coloured jacket approached from behind the counter on the far side of the room. His English accent was super cultured—he sounded how I imagined all rich English people sounded. There was something familiar about him.

Oh, crap. It was the young guy I'd snapped going through Mrs Valentine's drawers, the one with the choco-late-brown eyes. He had the longest lashes and a few freckles scattered across his nose, which hadn't been apparent in the photos. Unfortunately, he was even better looking in real life. I didn't know why, but it was always disappointing to find out someone attractive was a criminal—not that I knew he had done anything wrong, but he might have.

"Um, just looking. I've recently moved here from Australia, and I was wanting something for my bedroom." Would he think I was coming onto him by mentioning my bedroom? Should I have said living room? Crap.

"Are you after a watercolour, pastel, or oil painting? And do you have a subject in mind?"

"I'm not quite sure." I glanced around at the paintings. "Hmm, I think a typical English landscape would be nice, or architecture, like a village scene. Something with colour."

He looked at my raincoat, then down to my galoshes and grinned. "I see." He looked up at me again, mirth shining from his eyes. "Why don't you have a wander around, and if you see anything you like, just let me know. There's this room and two more through that doorway." He pointed to the right of his reception desk.

"Great, thanks." I gave him a smile, then ambled around

the room, taking in each painting as if I were serious. So, who was he, and why had he been in Mrs Valentine's drawers? I couldn't believe someone so respectable was a criminal. But then, Knight hadn't liked him, so there must be something to it. That was probably how attractive people got away with crime: no one wanted to believe they'd do something unforgivable, so they looked the other way.

I finished perusing all the paintings in the first room and made my way into the second. Whilst the first room had been landscapes, this room was a combination of portraits and nudes. One particularly striking pastel painting was of a young man sitting on a bed, from the front, a sheet covering his lower half, head bowed, eyes closed. Morning sun shone through a window to highlight his face and nicely muscled arms from the side. There was such atmosphere and calm about the picture. He looked as if he was relishing the peace before the chaos of the day snatched the quiet moments.

The signature at the bottom said "Ida Valentine." Oh, wow, Mrs Valentine had done this. She was really talented.

I felt a presence behind me. "Do you like it?"

I jumped, then turned. "Oh, hi. Yes. It's gorgeous."

It was the brown-eyed guy. "Did I scare you?" I nodded. "Sorry."

"That's okay. Do you have a lot of Ida Valentine's work in here?"

"A few, but they always sell quickly. She's been one of our bestsellers for the past couple of years. Her work will be worth a lot in the future—it's already in a handful of stately homes and galleries around Europe. This one's actually a bargain, but she believes in being fair to as many people as possible. We've tried to tell her people are happy to pay a premium for her work, but she won't hear of charging more."

I turned to look at the picture. The price was seven hundred pounds. It wasn't a bargain in my world, but whatever—it was still a lovely picture that would look good hanging above my bed—and how much was someone's talent and years of honing it worth? I bit my lip. Was I really considering dropping that much money on a piece of art? And it wasn't even that big, maybe fifty centimetres by ninety. I wouldn't normally, but something about it called to me, insisting I buy it. Maybe the universe was trying to tell me something. But seven hundred was a lot of money, and in pounds, no less. That was like a gazillion Australian dollars.

I surprised us both when I said over my shoulder, "I'll take it." His eyes widened. Maybe he'd thought I was a tyre kicker, and usually in art galleries and antique shops I was because I couldn't really afford to spend money on wants rather than needs.

He grinned. "I'll get it wrapped up for you."

Thunder cracked outside, making me wince. "Um, I walked. Can I pay now and collect it when it's not raining?"

"Why don't I have it delivered?"

"How much will that be? Sorry, but I'm stretching things buying it as it is." My smile was a touch embarrassed. I was sure rich people came in here all the time and dropped thousands without a second's worry. What was I doing buying this thing?

"It's on the house, as long as you live nearby. Which I'm assuming you do since you walked." He smiled. "I'll go wrap this. If you'd like to keep looking around, go for it. You can pay when you leave."

"Okay, thanks." He went to the first room, and I continued to the third, which was a mixture of abstract and black and white photography. Not my thing. I mean, some of the pictures were interesting, even pretty, but I enjoyed gazing at things I recognised, and I wasn't in the mood for photographs—more irony, but you could have too much of a good thing. Besides, I could take my own awesome photos and get them framed if I really wanted. I had a couple of my own shots up at home, in Sydney.

As I approached the reception desk, I realised I was going to have to give him my proper name and my real address. That wasn't very undercover. It was kind of stupid, actually. But then again, if he were a criminal, he would probably be wary of everyone. I wouldn't put it past him to research me. If I gave him false information, I'd look untrustworthy. So, I made a decision: I was going to try and get his trust after all. But how would I find out more about him if I just left with my picture?

He looked up from packaging the painting. "I didn't get your name. I'm Patrick."

"Hi, Patrick. I'm Lily."

"That's a pretty name." He blushed, then cleared his throat. "Will that be cash or card?"

"Card, thanks. I don't normally carry seven hundred pounds around." I laughed. "I usually only need enough for a cappuccino."

"Oh, yeah? Which café do you go to?"

Hmm, was he leading up to asking me out? I hoped so because I needed info, and he *was* kind of cute. There was nothing that said I couldn't enjoy doing my undercover work.

Maybe I should name a café I didn't go to, just in case he stalked me later. Plus, if anything weird went down between us, there would be no bad memories attached to Costa. "Deli De Luca."

"That's a nice café. They have a great selection of soups."

I blinked. Soup? Who cared about soup? I mean, soup was yummy and had its place, but cafes were supposed to be about coffee and sweet things, and maybe toasted sandwiches. I was rethinking wanting him to ask me out. Maybe Angelica could solve this case without my assistance.

"Lily?"

"Ah, sorry. I have a habit of drifting off into the ether."

He laughed and shook his head. "Don't worry about it." He leaned the securely wrapped picture against the side of the desk. "Done. I'll just put your card through the reader and get you to write your address here." He handed me a large hardcover notebook and pen. I gave him my credit card and then wrote down my details. I hoped Angelica wouldn't be mad at me for doing this. Was I putting her and Olivia at risk by drawing him to our place? But maybe he wasn't a witch, just a run-of-the-mill criminal. Or maybe he wasn't a criminal at all, and he'd had a good reason for rooting around in Mrs Valentine's stuff. I had hope, although it was probably misplaced.

"Great. All done. And congratulations on your new artwork. I'll see if we can get it delivered tomorrow. Will someone be home?"

"Um, there should be. If I'm not there, I'm sure my housemate could be." Olivia was studying, so it was likely she was going to be home, but if she wasn't, I'd be able to be there. If Angelica had any PIB work for me, she'd understand my need to stay home and wait for the painting.

"Okay, we'll see you tomorrow then. Good luck in the rain."

"Ah, yeah, thanks." I laughed. "And thanks for all your help, Patrick."

"It was my pleasure, Lily." He held eye contact for way too long, and I blushed. It did feel good that someone was showing some kind of interest after the William debacle. A girl had her ego to maintain, after all.

"Bye." I turned and walked out into a downpour. Hooray for big yellow raincoats, umbrellas, and purple galoshes. For once in my life, I was prepared.

With a bit of luck, I'd be ready for whatever tomorrow threw at me too. Unfortunately, we Bianchis had never been known for our good luck.

CHAPTER 9

After I got home and dried off, I went straight to see Olivia—it was confession time, and I didn't know who else to tell. It was so awesome to have her living right next to me. She'd only just arrived, but the house felt cosier with her in it. I never thought I'd be happy to live with two other people after living alone for so long, but it was actually nice.

I knocked on her door.

"Come in."

She was sitting on her bed, leaning against the headboard, a paperback in her lap. "How's it going?"

I sat on the chair next to her desk, tension knotting my shoulders. I knew I wasn't just here for a social call. "Not too shabby. I went to the Westerham Art Society's gallery today, and I bought a picture."

Her eyes widened. "Oh. Was it a print or an original?"

I laughed, pretty sure that was her attempt at subtly asking if I could afford it. "An original, by Mrs Valentine. And before you say anything, it was seven hundred pounds, but I had to buy it. It called to me."

She raised her brows. "Called to you?"

I nodded, then joked, "Ah huh. It hiss-whispered, 'Buy me now. Buy me now.' Like in a scary movie."

She grinned and rolled her eyes. "Very funny. You almost had me, though. I'm sure witches could spell their own paintings to call out to people. You should try it."

"Yes, but one thing at a time. And maybe I should learn to draw better first. No one wants saggy-balls paintings." We laughed.

She did make a good point about me learning new spells. There were so many things for me to try, yet I hardly ever had time to get down to creating any new spells. I was still behind on making one to protect Olivia from telling people about witches. I should get onto that soon. I also needed to learn some attacking spells and detection spells, to see if someone had protection spells on them that would bounce my attacking spell back to me. Sheesh, this stuff was complicated.

Olivia put her book on the bed, wriggled to the edge, then stood. "So, where is it?"

"I don't have it yet. It was raining, and I walked, so they're going to deliver tomorrow sometime. I'm probably going to be here, but if Angelica calls any meetings, I may have to go out. If that happens, will you be here to answer the door?"

"Yep. I have nothing planned, and I have an exam in two days, so I was going to study. I'm kind of over it, but I don't want to fail."

"You're going to ace it. I just know."

"Thanks. Well, if I don't, it won't be for lack of trying." She sat back down, cocked her head, and narrowed her eyes. "What aren't you telling me, miss?"

So, here was the part I didn't want to talk about, but I had to tell someone, in case my plan went downhill in a red Ferrari with no brakes, and I needed backup. "I need to tell you something, but you can't tell Angelica, or anyone, including Beren, and especially not my brother. If you don't want to keep a secret from them, it's okay. I don't have to tell you."

"What the hell, Lily? You can't say all that, then not tell me. I can keep a secret, unless it's something really bad, like you want to kill yourself or something."

"Oh my God, no! I can assure you, as shitty as my life gets at times, I would never do that. Once you're gone, you're gone, and I like being here, even if it's painful sometimes. I can't leave without falling in love at least once, can I?"

She grinned. "Nope, definitely not. So, what's the big secret?"

I hesitated. Should I get her to swear on a spell? It would guarantee her compliance, but then, she was the closest thing I had to a best friend here, and I should trust her. Hmm, definitely no spell. "I'm trying to go undercover."

She scrunched up her face. "What?"

"I probably shouldn't be telling you this, but Knight, the fox, told us about a man he didn't trust because he was searching through Mrs Valentine's drawers in the barn conversion. So I took photos, and I saw the guy in the past, doing just what Knight said he had been. Anyway, I was just scouting things out at the art society, because I think they stand to inherit a lot of her money."

"But aren't Beren and William questioning the art society people anyway?"

"Ah, yes. William and *Dana* are." I ground my back teeth together. *Deep breaths, Lily.*

"We hate Dana. She's such a witch." She nodded.

"Yes, we do." We both smiled. Joking about it made it easier... sort of. "Anyway, when I went to the gallery today, guess who was there to sell me the drawing?"

Her mouth opened wide, and she made a shocked noise. "No way! The guy from your photo?"

"Yep. And he's about our age and attractive. So I'm going to try and get to know him better. I see a few more trips to the gallery in my future. I don't want to come on too strong because he'd probably run a mile, but I'm thinking of asking him out for coffee, to chat about art. I'll use the excuse that I don't have many friends here yet."

"Good idea. But is he dangerous? I mean, if he was stealing from her. Oh my God. What if he's a witch?" Her eyes widened.

"I don't know."

"Is there a way to tell?"

"I have no idea. I've been meaning to ask Angelica, but I

keep forgetting." Gah, there was so much to do and find out. Being a witch was more taxing than a full-time job. "I just want to make sure we find out what happened to Mrs Valentine and Knight. The longer she's missing, the more I think she must be dead. If they were willing to kill a fox who only had a limited way of communicating, I imagined killing the source of the information would be a necessity if they were trying to hide something, and if they wanted her money, well, that wouldn't happen unless she was dead."

Lightning flashed outside, and two seconds later, thunder boomed, and the rain pelted harder. I shivered. We looked at each other.

Olivia said, "Yikes."

"Why don't we do something pleasant?"

"Like what?"

"I bought ingredients for chocolate chip cookies the other day. Why don't we go and bake up a storm?" The thunder cracked again, rattling the window. "Come on. A storm of cookies is much better than sitting here waiting for a bolt of lightning to crash through the window."

"You have a point. Let's go."

THAT NIGHT, OLIVIA AND I ATE DINNER TOGETHER— Angelica still hadn't returned from work by seven, and we were starving, even after our cookie binge that afternoon. We then retired to the living room, the fire cheering up the fireplace because the temperature had dropped to twelve degrees. Olivia laughed at me for being cold, but I still hadn't acclimatised. She sat there in T-shirt and shorts, and I had on tracksuit pants and a jumper. The table lamps were our light source, and it was like being embraced in a giant cuddle. This was definitely my favourite room in the house.

We were each sitting in an armchair near the fire, reading, when Angelica entered. "Good evening, ladies. How was your day?"

We answered simultaneously, "Good, thanks."

She came all the way over to us and stood next to my chair. Her poker face, carefully neutral, spoke volumes and did the opposite of what it was supposed to. I sat up straight. "What's wrong, Ma'am? Did something happen?"

"No, dear. But I have the results of Knight's autopsy."

That was unexpected. Sadness, thick and stifling, coated my heart, and I dropped my head for a moment, remembering both Knight and Mrs Valentine. Angelica waited until I looked up before she continued.

"He died from choking, but it wasn't accidental. Someone spelled the food to swell once it was in his throat. It expanded and cut off his airway."

"What a horrible way to die. Bastards." I hoped whoever did this died the same way and suffered even more.

Olivia shook her head. "That's just terrible. Poor fox."

"Were you able to get the magical signature from the spell?" Surely something helpful had to come of the autopsy.

"As a matter of fact, we did, but it doesn't match anyone in our database."

"So now what?" This got more depressing by the minute.

"We'd love to get a read on the suspects' magic signatures, but unless we have more than a hunch, we don't have a good enough reason to test someone—it's the same with regular police and fingerprints. You can't just take people's prints for the hell of it."

"Also, another question," I said. "How do we tell if someone's a witch? I mean, I can't tell the difference. Is there a way to tell without asking?"

"Good question. There are two ways. One is if you feel that telltale tingle of someone performing magic, you can cast a spell asking to see who it is, and their aura will become visible. Everyone has a similar-coloured aura, which is the same golden hue as our magic signatures. Our auras flare brighter when we perform magic because as well as using energy when you cast a spell, you also draw energy from the pool of magic. The other way to tell if someone is a witch is to develop your second sight, and then you'll be able to tell just by looking at them."

I smiled. "You know what my next question is."

She laughed. "Of course. You need to focus on the spot at the top of your nose, between your eyes. Then send a bit of magic into it, and it will give you other sight. You'll not only see witch auras but human ones too."

"Wow, okay."

"But be careful not to draw too much power because you might burn your third eye out forever. And if you draw way too much power, you could fry your brain." She smiled, as if she'd just imparted a secret cake recipe. What was wrong with her?

"Right. I'm surprised witches try anything for the first time. I wonder how many died figuring this out." I shook my head.

"You know what they say, dear: no guts, no glory."

"More like, no guts, no gory." I giggled, and so did Olivia. She was a true friend.

Angelica managed a tiny upward curl of her lips, but that was it. I stopped myself from insisting it was funny, but only just. "Okay, time for me to head to bed. We've a big day tomorrow. I'll be compiling reports from the rest of the interviews and deciding how to deploy our *valuable* resources." Her mouth twisted in a manner that suggested she was thoroughly unimpressed by Drake's decree.

"So I won't have to come in tomorrow?"

"Not at this stage, Lily, but probably the day after."

And wasn't that fantastic news. I wouldn't have to see William and his future ex ex. And I'd be home to receive my sketch. "Okay, sounds good. Sleep well."

"Goodnight, ladies."

"Night, Ma'am." At least Olivia had to call her Ma'am too. I would have been really offended if it were only me— we were at home, after all. At work, I could understand. Was it so she could keep some kind of distance between herself and others? Yet another thing to figure out later.

About an hour after Ma'am retired, Olivia and I said our goodnights. I went to have my shower—Olivia show-ered in the morning—then I snuggled up in bed with one of

Mum's diaries. I'd neglected my hunt for clues because life had been so busy. A little voice deep inside me admitted I was afraid of what I might find. Last time I'd accidentally crossed paths with my parents' history, I'd seen them in my camera, and it was like they'd died all over again.

The desperate ache that could never be soothed invaded my skin, my blood, my heart, my marrow until I throbbed with it. I sightlessly stared at the page. A tear landed on it, smudging the ink. I started and quickly wiped it off. I didn't want to ruin anything she'd left me, and what if something crucial was there, and then I couldn't read it because I'd cried over the whole thing?

I grabbed a tissue from my bedside table, wiped my tears, and blew my nose. Be strong. *What if they're waiting for you? And even if they're not, think of James's little one.* He or she would be in the world in a few months, and I wanted them to be safe.

My eyes stayed dry, and I read until I was too tired to keep my eyes open. I read the same pages over and over until a brilliant yet scary idea came to me, but I was too tired to do anything with it except acknowledge it was there.

I put the diary under my pillow, turned off my lamp, and promptly fell asleep.

CHAPTER 10

T he next morning, I woke up early and dressed straight away—I didn't want to be in my pyjamas when the courier showed up with my painting. I was surprised at how excited I was to get it. Not only was the subject stunning but quiet, calm, yet strong and purposeful. And don't ask me how I got all that from the painting; I just did.

After I received it, I planned to take a shot of it and find out if the Westerham Art Society had a Facebook page, and if so, I'd share it there, maybe tag Patrick. Although, that might look too desperate. I could just thank him for helping me choose such a gorgeous work of art. Hmm, that sounded less weirdo and much cooler.

It was 8:00 a.m., and I was having my coffee when the doorbell rang. I hurried and checked the peephole. Oh my God. This was unexpected. I opened the door. "Patrick! I didn't expect you to deliver it." I grinned. My undercover work was off to a smashing start.

He smiled, showing a couple of well-placed dimples. "I wanted to make sure it got to you safely." The painting, although not huge, looked awkward in his arms.

I stepped aside. "Please, come in."

He stepped into the vestibule. "Which way?"

"Go left and then into the first door on the left." Yes, I was putting it in my bedroom, but no, I wasn't going to get him to take it there. That totally would have screamed desperate.

I followed him in, and he set it down carefully on one of the Chesterfields. "Nice place."

"Thanks. It's not mine. It's my... aunt's. She's been in the house by herself for years, and when I decided to move here, she insisted I move in with her until I could afford a place of my own. It's worked out quite well, actually."

"Nice. I love your cool Australian accent. Were you born there?"

"Yes, lived there my whole life until I came here a few weeks ago. What about you? Have you always lived in Westerham?"

"No. I was born in London, and when I was five, my parents moved us to Ireland for ten years, and then we ended up here. Dad's owned different galleries. He actually manages the art society's stuff, and I work in the shop. Mum acquires the art, and we have two other board members who come up with marketing ideas and organise shows."

"Oh, hello. I thought I heard the doorbell." Olivia had finished her shower and was dressed and curious.

I smirked. "This is Patrick, from the gallery. Patrick, this is my friend Olivia."

His expression was kind of confused, but then he smiled. Did he recognise her from somewhere? "Hi. Nice to meet you."

"Likewise. I'm dying to look at the picture. Can you open it now, Lily, please?" She clasped her hands under her chin, begging.

I laughed. "Okay, yeah. In fact, I'd love to see it again. I've been looking forward to it since yesterday."

Patrick grinned. Was he putting it on, or was he truly happy to see this go to a good home? I made my way to the Chesterfield and knelt in front of it, looking for the edge of the tape securing the box. He'd only wrapped it in paper in the shop, but he'd obviously thought that wasn't enough when transporting. It was in a narrow cardboard box. I found the edge of the tape and picked at it with my fingernail. Grrr, why is tape extra sticky when you don't want it to be? Stupid tape. I dug my nail in harder, frustration whispering at me to just rip the box open. *I'm with you, buddy, but not in front of company.* I didn't want Patrick to think I was a box-ripping psycho.

The tape finally gave, and I ripped it off and opened the thin foldy-outy bit at the top of the box, then slid the framed nude out. I stood and held it in front of me, facing Olivia and Patrick. "Ta-da!"

Olivia's mouth dropped open. Then she grinned. She

leaned forward and stared at the picture. "That's gorgeous! Wow. I'm jealous. Mrs Valentine really was... is talented." She didn't look at my face, obviously realising her mistake.

I glanced at Patrick, and he hadn't seemed to notice Olivia's slip up. I turned the painting around and held my arms out, having a good look. I smiled. It really was beautiful. "I can't wait to put this up in my room."

"Do you need some help?" Patrick looked at me as if it was normal to ask to go into a stranger's bedroom.

"Um, no. I'll be fine, but I would like to shout you a coffee. That is, if you have time over the next couple of days. You've been so helpful, bringing this here."

He smiled. "I'd love to have coffee with you, Lily, but it's my treat."

"Don't be silly. I owe you."

"You don't owe me. I never let a lady pay when I take her out."

I couldn't help my grin. He'd practically said it was a date. Not that I wanted to date, date him, but it was nice that a cute guy, regardless of the fact that he might be a criminal, wanted to ask me out. That sounded all kinds of wrong. Maybe I was more desperate for male company than I thought. "You're too nice, but seriously, my shout."

Olivia blew out a loud sigh. "Oh, for goodness' sake, Lily. Just let the man pay. If I have to listen to this much longer, I'll pay, just to get you two out of here."

"Touchy, much?" I asked, then laughed.

Olivia snorted and giggled. "I wasn't joking." She winked.

"I have time now, if you do, Lily. Café Deli De Luca?"

Wow, Patrick was more keen than I had guessed. "That would be awesome. I'll just take this upstairs and grab my bag. I carefully carried the picture up to my room. While I was getting my bag, I called Angelica. "Hi, Ma'am."

"Hello, Lily. You're calling early."

"Yes. I'm just going out for coffee with Patrick from the art gallery. We're having coffee at Deli De Luca."

"Patrick who happens to be on the board of directors?" Her voice had a definite bossy tone that suggested she may be about to put a kibosh on the whole thing.

"Yes, that Patrick. He seems nice enough. I won't be gone long. I'm pretty sure he has to go to work."

"I don't think this is a good idea, Lily. He could be involved in Mrs Valentine's disappearance."

"I know, but innocent until proven guilty, right? Plus, he's cute, and now that I have no hope with stupid William, I need to move on, and going for coffee with one guy is hardly going to be life altering." I slapped my hand over my mouth. Argh, I'd just admitted my feelings to Angelica. I'm sure she'd suspected—she wasn't stupid—but I was worried she'd think less of me or make fun of me for liking him. Or even worse, tell William how I felt.

She sighed. "Okay, but be careful. Patrick's a witch, so make sure your mind-protection spell is up."

Oh, wow. I hadn't seen that coming. "Will do, Ma'am. I'll call you when I get home."

"You do that, Lily. And, for the record, a blind person

could see how you feel about Will. I'm just glad you're finally opening up to me. I'll speak to you later."

My cheeks heated. Of course she knew. I was totally Captain Obvious. "Bye." The line cut off, and I slid my phone into my bag and took a deep breath, wiping all thoughts of William out of my mind. Then I walked downstairs, careful not to rush and seem too eager.

Patrick was waiting for me at the front door, which he opened. "After you, milady."

"Aw, thanks." *Take that, William. You're not the only one who's dating.* Something told me I wasn't dealing with this William rejection thing very well, but I didn't have the heart to admit it to myself, as I was having such a lovely morning. "Nice car."

A fairly new British-racing-green Jaguar two door sat in Angelica's driveway. Nice. That kind of car cost more than a Range Rover, and yes, I knew how much nice cars cost. One of my hobbies back in Sydney when I was bored was to google expensive cars to find what I'd like to buy when I got rich. I expected I'd never own one, at least not while they were newish. I'd have to wait twenty years, when they'd depreciated in value. Unless I wanted to live in the car, of course. I could always sell my apartment and live in a new Porsche. I laughed.

"What's so funny?" Patrick was standing next to the front passenger door, holding it open.

Ooh, what a gentleman. "Just thinking about how stupid I am. Nothing to see here. Nice car." I smiled.

He cocked his head to the side and looked at me, probably deciding whether going out for coffee with me was a good idea. "Thanks."

I slid into the seat, and he shut the door. A little burst of happiness unfurled inside me. It was the kind of joy that came from savouring the first mouthful of chocolate mousse. Okay, it wasn't that good, but close. It wasn't often someone went out of their way to treat me as if I was super special. My mouth watered. Oh dear. Think about chocolate mousse on an empty stomach, and that's what you got. Hopefully the café we were going to had chocolate mousse. Mmm.

Patrick started the car, put his arm around the back of my seat, and turned to look out the rear-view mirror to reverse down the driveway. It was such a masculine thing to do. I'd never seen a woman reverse like that, although it's probably happened. My dad used to do it. I remembered one time, we reversed down the street to a parking space, Dad with his arm around Mum's seat, his head turned towards my brother and me in the back seat. He looked so in control, capable, the doer of things like reversing so quickly, the gearbox whined. I sighed, sadness running up and nipping my heart, causing a jolt of pain. My memories were like a cute dog that wagged its tail and drew you in, but when you went in for the pat, it bit you.

Once we were on our way, I needed to fill the silence. I didn't know this guy well enough for quiet time to be comfortable. Was he regretting this "date" already? Had he wished he'd sent a courier to deliver the painting? I needed to say something, if only to shut off my chatty, irritating brain. "How long have you had this car?"

He patted the steering wheel with one hand and grinned. "Two months. And I've loved every minute of it. She does nought to sixty miles in three point five seconds. Would you like to see?" He put his foot down, and the car took off.

I gripped the door as I was pushed into my seat, but he eased off the power just as I had visions of us flying through the intersection and dying as we collided with a truck.

"Just joking. But you get the picture." He glanced at me as we stopped at the main road and waited to turn left.

"Yep, I definitely get the picture. No need to ever show me again."

"Don't worry, Lily. I would never put you in danger. I was in complete control."

Yeah, this time. I had enough danger in my life: I didn't need to increase my odds of dying young. I decided I'd walk home. He'd probably have to go straight to work, and that was in the opposite direction.

"So, how old are you, if you don't mind me asking." He made the turn and spared me a quick glance.

"Twenty-four. You?"

"Thirty. I figured you were about twenty-four."

Hmm, did I dare ask why? He made it sound as if it was for a bad reason. "You look way younger than thirty. So, how did you figure how old I was?"

He veered left at the village green and found a parking spot straight away. He cut the engine, then looked straight at me. "Don't take this the wrong way, but your aura isn't very strong, which indicates you don't have strong power, which is common in young witches. The more experience you have, the stronger your aura."

Okay, I was not expecting that. Was that normal for witches to just come out and talk about it? "Ah, okay, yeah. I'm pretty new at the whole witchy thing." No need to rub my pointy hat in it, though.

He smiled. "Hey, don't worry. You'll get there. Now, stay put." He opened his door and rushed around to my side to open mine. He was a crazy driver, but he knew how to charm... or maybe he was just good at opening doors. He wasn't so great on the compliments, come to think of it. Hopefully this wouldn't be for nothing, and I'd get some kind of information that would lead us to Mrs Valentine.

He locked the car, and we walked along the footpath. Deli De Luca was less than a minute away, and only a few doors down from Napoli E, the restaurant I'd gone to the other night with Olivia. I looked around, remembering I was still a hunted person. Stupid thug. I didn't see anything untoward, and since I had that alarm, I was sure I'd hear he was coming way before I saw him.

The café was also across the street from Costa. I looked longingly at my favourite haunt as we passed. Was it normal to feel guilty, as if I was cheating on Costa by going to Deli De Luca? *Oh, coffee gods, please forgive me, for I have sinned.* It was for a good cause, though.

I followed Patrick inside, and he found a table near the

specials board. We sat, and Patrick asked what I wanted. "Just a skim milk cappuccino, thanks."

"You're not eating?"

"I wasn't sure if you'd have time."

"I always have time for soup."

"Ah, okay. I'll get a chocolate-filled croissant then."

He ordered, then pinned me with his dark, enquiring gaze. "So, have you had a chance to visit the National Gallery?"

"Yes. I went there a few weeks ago. I was so excited to see the Cannalettos. He's one of my favourite artists."

"You have good taste. What about Claude Lorrain?"

"Ah, I haven't heard of him. I'm not really an expert. I just know what I like when I see it, and then I get to know who the artist is. But I plan on spending more time familiarising myself with the artwork in England." I was trying not to sound clueless, but I didn't think it was working.

He lifted his chin and actually looked down his nose at me, and I tried not to feel stupid. "I have some books you can borrow if you're serious about learning." Was that condescension in his tone or an actual offer to help? One could never tell—these English all had pretty good poker faces. Admittedly, Ma'am had the best one, but everyone else had a reasonable level of skill.

Time to change the subject and get back on track. "You know the painting I bought? Is it by the same Ida Valentine who runs the art classes here?"

He stared at me for a beat too long before answering. "I believe it is. Have you done any of her classes?"

"Only two. I'm actually quite terrible, but I suppose nothing comes well without practice. What about you?"

He laughed. "No. I'm hopeless. I prefer to look rather than do." He leaned towards me and lowered his voice. "Did you hear she's missing?"

"No, but I did get an email saying the rest of term classes had been cancelled, and that they're giving refunds for the untaken lessons. I hope she's okay. She was really nice and quite an interesting person."

His brow creased. "Did you know her well?"

I shook my head. "No. I'd only seen her in my two classes. That was it, but she was so vivacious and, as evidenced by the drawing I bought, very talented."

Our drinks and food arrived, and we started eating. Patrick's pretentious pinky finger stuck out as he spooned his soup into his mouth. He was too cultured to slurp. My pastry was delicious, and I resisted the urge to murmur my joy—I didn't want a repeat of Café Castel in Paris, when Beren and William thought we were re-enacting *When Sally Met Harry*. Unfortunately, the coffee wasn't as good as Costa's. Well, maybe other people would say it was good, but I didn't like bitter coffee. I liked it smooth. If I had to come here again, I'd try the hot chocolate. Someone else was drinking one, and I could smell its deliciousness.

Not much conversation flowed during the rest of the meal, and what chat there was leant towards the mundane. We even talked about London weather versus Sydney weather—definitely scraping the bottom of the conversation barrel. When the bill came, Patrick insisted on paying.

"But I asked you." I wasn't someone who thought it was always the guy's duty to pay.

"Put your wallet away, Lily. Honestly, I can more than afford it. You wouldn't want to hurt a guy's ego, would you?"

"Ah, no. That's the last thing I'd want to do." I think he missed my sarcasm.

"Good. If you're that keen to pay, we'll just have to do this again another day. I have your number. I'll call you." He smiled.

Okay, there was absolutely nothing wrong with his ego. I bit my lip and tried not to laugh. "Sounds good. I'll hear from you soon."

"You can count on it." He put his hand on my shoulder and kissed my cheek, lingering momentarily. I know this shouldn't be my reaction to an attractive-looking guy kissing my cheek, but I had to resist scrunching my face. It was such a meh feeling having his lips on my face. He pulled away. "I'll see you soon."

We walked out of the café. He headed for his car, and I turned left, back towards home. I constantly looked over my shoulder, wary despite the agents tailing me and the alarm. There was always the chance he'd pop out of nowhere. And if he'd gone rogue, who had they replaced him and his dead brother with? I almost felt like the Pied Piper of the crime world: I was walking around with potentially five people tailing me. I snorted. It was rather ridiculous.

Knowing I was being watched, at least by the agents, made me self-conscious. My nose was itchy, and I couldn't even scratch it. What if they thought I was picking it? I'd never live that down. I bet agents talked amongst themselves about all the gross stuff they'd seen their targets do. No more dawdling for me. I picked up my pace, almost jogging, which got me home fairly quickly.

As soon as I got in the door and locked it, I heaved a relieved breath in and out, scratched my nose, then texted Angelica. *Home safe and sound. Any news?*

Maybe they'd had a breakthrough in the short time I'd been gone. I didn't really believe that, but you never knew. My phone dinged. *Glad to hear it. And no. No breakthrough. Have to go now.* She was never one for idle conversation.

"Hey, you're back already." Olivia stood at the bottom of the stairs, a cup of tea in her hand.

I gave her a rundown of the "date," and she asked, "Do you think he had a reason to kidnap her or hurt her?"

I shook my head. "He's kind of irritating but in a harmless way. I'm probably wasting my time pursuing this angle. Besides, William and *Dana* have already interviewed him, and if they'd found anything untoward, they would have mentioned it."

She smirked. "Are you always going to say that woman's name like you're a cranky four-year-old and she took your favourite toy?"

"Probably, so you'd better get used to it." I stuck my tongue out, and she laughed.

I hung the picture, admired it for a while, then read one of my mother's diaries. Olivia studied but had an afternoon-tea get-together with her mother, so I was left bored later that afternoon. The morning had been fairly sunny, but dark clouds rolled in, the pitter-patter of rain making me happy I was warm and dry inside. My eyes grew heavy, tiredness whispering how good a nap would be. I yawned and gave in, tucking the diary under my pillow before conking out.

❦

KNOCKING SOUNDED IN THE DISTANCE. *HUH?* I OPENED MY eyes. Ew: wet pillow under my cheek. I swiped the dribble off my face. *Knock, knock.* Oh, it was my bedroom door. "Yeah, come in." My voice came out a croaky mess. I cleared my throat as Angelica entered.

"Hello, lazy bones." She smirked.

"What time is it?"

She looked at her watch. "Six thirty." She looked above my head, her eyes wide. "Is that the picture you bought yesterday?"

"Yes. Mrs Valentine did it. I don't know. It just spoke to me."

Her eyes widened. "What did it say?"

I squeezed my eyes shut for a moment, then looked at her. Was she serious? "No. I was speaking figuratively. I just had this overwhelming urge to buy it when I saw it."

"Ah." She nodded.

Wait, what? "Can witches spell paintings to actually talk to people?"

"Yes. It's a classic witch-spy move to leave a message in artwork for a colleague."

"Then wouldn't it be more like a video?"

"The picture doesn't change, Lily. Honestly, that would be too obvious."

I sighed. Of course it would be—stupid me. I resisted an eye-roll.

She approached the picture, and I scooted towards the foot of my bed and placed my feet on the floor, to get out of her way. She opened her hand and placed her palm parallel with the picture, so she was almost touching the glass. My scalp prickled.

"What are you doing?"

"Just a moment, dear. It's not polite to talk to a witch when she's performing magic."

I mouthed "sorry" because, well, it was impolite for me to talk right now. I was a fast learner. I bit my fingernail while I waited.

She dropped her hand to her side and turned around. "Well, Lily, you've stumbled upon something very interesting. And it might be an important clue. If it's not, we can at least arrest someone for committing a crime."

My heart raced. I'd actually found a clue? But hang on. Was I about to lose my painting? "What did you find? And please don't tell me you need the painting as evidence."

"I'm afraid so, dear. I'm going to send it to evidence." She waved her hand towards the picture, and it disappeared.

What? Noooo! I frowned. *Bye, bye, Mrs Valentine's artwork. Bye, bye, seven hundred pounds.* I wasn't sure which hurt more. "Can I have it back when all this is over?"

"Yes, don't worry. And we'll be careful with it while it's in our care." She turned to leave.

"Hang on a minute! You can't just tell me I've found a clue, whisk it away, then go. Please don't leave me in suspense." I wasn't too ashamed to beg. I clasped my hands under my chin.

She shook her head. "Don't worry. I won't keep you waiting long. Why don't we have dinner first, and then I'll call everyone to the conference room. That's why I came to get you. Olivia's downstairs waiting to eat." She smirked and walked out the door. Her voice was quiet but still reached me from the hallway. "Patience is a virtue, Lily."

Patience smatience. She was going to leave me hanging over dinner. How cruel could someone be? Argh. She totally got her kicks from torturing people. Why couldn't she save the mean stuff for the criminals?

I raced downstairs, said hi to Olivia, and ate quickly. I finished my beef in black bean sauce stir-fry in record time. I magicked my plate and utensils into the dishwasher, sat up straight, and stared at Angelica—I stopped just short of lolling my tongue out and panting. She skilfully ignored me. Olivia snorted. "What are you doing?"

"Waiting. Ma'am said Mrs Valentine's picture is spelled, but she won't tell me how and why until after dinner. My lovely work of art is now in evidence at the PIB." I pouted but didn't shift my gaze.

Ma'am narrowed her eyes and matched my stare. "Are you going to look at me with that face until I tell you?"

I nodded.

She sighed. "Fine. I'm only giving in because it's been a long day, and my favourite TV show is on in an hour. Come on, then." She flicked her hand at the table, and her dirty stuff disappeared. Her phone appeared in her hand, and she dialled someone. "Beren, be a dear and get the team together. Yes, now." She hung up, and her phone vanished. She stood and gave me one last look. Then she was gone.

I pressed my lips together, trying not to smile. I'd won! Yes, the prize wasn't anything that fantastic, but what if the painting led us to Mrs Valentine? It was also handy to know Ma'am wasn't immune to the effects of my stubbornness. "Be back soon, Liv."

"You have to tell me everything."

I stood. "Will do." Then I conjured my doorway and stepped through.

CHAPTER 11

No one had wasted time getting here. When I entered the PIB conference room, James, Millicent, William, Beren, and Dana the Piranha were there. She was sitting next to William, and as soon as she saw me, she leaned over and whispered something to him. He smiled and looked at Millicent. Whatever. She better not be trash-talking my sister-in-law, or I was going to break her nose. I sighed. Fair enough: I'd never break her nose. I knew it, anyone who knew me knew it, but I could still want to do it, couldn't I?

But then William looked at me and scowled. What the hell had I done now? I gave a little headshake and shut the door.

I approached the table, focussing on my brother. "Hey," I said, then sat next to Beren.

James looked at me. "I hear you may have found us some evidence."

I shrugged and looked at Ma'am. "I have no idea, but Ma'am's going to enlighten us. She told me there was a spell on it. Then she made me sit through dinner and suffer."

Angelica smirked. "I've told Lily that patience is a necessary attribute."

James grinned. "Welcome to my world, sis." He'd probably been on the receiving end of her holding-back-information-for-fun tendencies.

"So, can we find out now? Pretty please?"

"Okay, Lily. I've made you suffer long enough." Her smile slipped, and her work poker face was back. "Lily did some of her own snooping around."

Someone sniggered. "Since when do agents snoop?" It was the piranha, of course. "We investigate."

Ma'am looked at her. Her expression didn't change, but Piranha got the message and schooled her face to neutral. So, me being a civilian meant I was a joke? She probably didn't know about my awesome photography skill, and I hoped she'd never find out. I didn't trust her, and if she wanted to feel superior to me, good on her. It just showed she probably felt threatened. That or I was delusional and trying to make myself feel better. Either way, it was a win for me to hang onto that line of thought. I also made a mental note to confirm with Angelica that Piranha wouldn't find out about my talent.

"Thanks to Lily, we now have another piece of the puzzle." She gave me a nod, and I smiled. "The pastel painting Lily bought was done by our missing person—Mrs Valentine. The picture contains an enticement spell, woven in after creation."

Huh? If that was what it sounded like, maybe that's why I felt the pull to buy it. My brow wrinkled. I hated being ripped off.

James said, "Do we know who cast the spell? If it were someone at the gallery, we would need to bring charges against them for enticement to buy resulting in an exchange of funds under false pretences."

"No, but we now have an excuse to test every member of the Westerham Art Society's magic signature to find out." Angelica's grin was smug.

"But what if Mrs Valentine did it? When Millicent and I interviewed Henry, he said she always won the art shows she entered, much to the dismay of one of the other artists. The woman sounded like she hated Mrs Valentine. I wonder if she was another witch who knew what she'd been doing?"

Millicent tapped the desk, thinking. "You could be right, Lily. Maybe we should pay this woman a visit before we go stirring up the board of directors. If we haven't exhausted all other avenues and one of them complains to Mr Pembleton, we'll all be in trouble."

Ma'am's nostrils flared—the only indication she was annoyed. "Good idea, Agent Bianchi. Make an appointment, and you and Lily can interview her. James, do you have the time to go along? We could use your lie-detecting skills, and surely you can be spared for thirty minutes?" There was obviously some kind of tug of war going on between Ma'am and the duck, and James was in the middle. I really hoped it was a competition Angelica won.

James nodded. "I'll see what I can do."

"Agent DuPree, you also have something to report." Angelica pinned her nephew with her stare. She wasn't always this formal. Was this to impress Agent Piranha?

"Yes, Ma'am. The Westerham Art Society stands to inherit the majority of Mrs Valentine's assets, which, according to her brother, were fairly substantial, but we've checked ownership details on her property. She owns it but owes at least half its value to Barclays Bank. The final sum will still be considerable, and I've heard that the art society is looking to find bigger premises, but I don't think that's motivation enough to kill someone."

"And don't forget: you don't have a dead body. It will be a long time before probate can go through." I hated Piranha, but she made a fair point.

I mused aloud. "Maybe they're not desperate for the money yet, and they don't want her body found because it will lead to them? They could be biding their time."

Ma'am nodded. "Agent Bianchi"—she was looking at Millicent—"make that appointment, then update me." She stood. "Meeting's over. Dismissed." Instead of popping away, she stayed seated, staring at the far wall.

Beren leaned towards me. He didn't quite whisper, but his voice was low. "A little birdie told me you went on a date. Spill."

"Is nothing private in this place?"

He grinned. Angelica told Will and me you went out with one of our suspects."

"He doesn't seem like much of a criminal." I didn't need to confirm whether I liked him or not. Let William think I was having hot dates with other men. At least I wouldn't seem like such a loser.

"You know what I think?" He looked entirely too smug.

"No, and I don't want to know." We still hadn't gotten to the bottom of this, and I had a feeling I could get some kind of good information from Patrick if I stuck with the dating thing long enough. Although maybe he'd get sick of me before I was done.

"You're no fun, Miss Bianchi. But I'm going to tell you anyway."

He was just about to tell me, when William said, "Bye," and he and Piranha popped away. Together. They were certainly spending a lot of time with each other. I swallowed a growl and reminded myself I didn't care and that I had a date with Patrick in the near future. Yeah, great. Did that make me a bad person? I didn't like him, like him—looks could only take someone so far. His attitude was… irritating, and he thought it was funny to drive like a maniac and scare me. Maybe he had a super nice side I was yet to see. It could just be that he felt he had to impress me? We'd see.

Beren cleared his throat. "As I was saying, I think you're dating him to get information. He doesn't seem your type."

"And who is my type, smarty pants?"

That was the opening he'd been looking for. If I was

half as smart as I thought I was, I would have just ignored him.

"William."

I gave him the dirtiest look I could. "If I didn't like you so much, B, I would make your life very uncomfortable." I could come up with an ants-in-the-pants spell. Surely it couldn't be too hard. I smirked.

All of a sudden, he didn't look so sure. "May I remind you that whatever you do, I can do too, and worse?"

I lowered my voice, made it menacing. "When you least expect it, expect it." I squinted my eyes in what I hoped was a dangerous look, but all it did was make his lips quirk up.

"For the record, I'm really scared. But just so you know, if anything weird happens to me, you'd better watch out." He waggled his fingers, pretending to cast a spell.

"Ha ha. I'm terrified, witch boy."

"Are you two finished?" Ma'am asked, her eyebrow raised.

Oops. I'd forgotten Ma'am, James, and Millicent were still there. Good thing, though, because I had a question to ask, which I hadn't wanted to ask in front of Piranha. "Sorry. I do have a question, Ma'am. I feel like we're not getting very far with this investigation, and that if we found Mrs Valentine, we could finally get to the bottom of every-thing. I think I should go to where she was last seen alive and take some photos. It would be a slow process, but I could potentially follow where she went. I'd have to stop frequently and maybe have to backtrack down roads, but this seems like our best option."

She smoothed a hand over her bun and shared a look with James. Had they already spoken about this? "Lily, we were afraid it would come to this, and you're right. We've had trouble finding clues as to her whereabouts: it's as if she's vanished off the face of the earth. But we have a… problem. I have to meet with Drake Pemberton in five minutes, but James will go home with you and fill you in. If you have any questions he can't answer, I'll be home later." Her voice lost some authority at the end and sounded almost resigned, or was that worried?

I bit my lip. Whatever James had to tell me was probably not going to be great. I took a deep breath. I could handle whatever came my way; I was the queen of receiving bad news. "Okay, Ma'am." I stood. "Come on, James. Let's get this over with. Bye, B, Millicent, Ma'am." I waved and made my doorway.

Ma'am's reception room was nice and warm. Olivia must have turned on the central heating, which was weird for an English person. I was pretty sure it had to be blizzarding before they felt the cold, and it was still ten degrees. Oh, what an awesome summer.

As I left the reception room, James came in behind me. He shut and locked the door before joining me in the sitting room. We sat in our usual place on one of the Chesterfields. It seemed like the unofficial bad-news-imparting spot. "So, big brother, what's news?"

"Nothing good, I'm afraid." He waved one arm in an arc, and the back of my neck tingled with power. "Privacy spell, so no one can hear us."

This was starting off well. "So, what did you want to tell me?"

"We'll get you to track where Mrs Valentine went, but we can't tell anyone, and we can't use it as evidence later."

"Okay. That doesn't sound too bad, except for the why."

He bit his bottom lip. "We don't want anyone else to know about your talent. All the photos you took for our previous cases have been destroyed. We've wiped the memories of everyone who knew they existed, although most of them didn't know who took the photos. We just don't want anything leading back to you."

I scrunched up my face. This didn't make sense. "But why? We were already keeping it quiet. If no one knew who took them, what does it matter?"

"Because your magic signature is on them. If someone really wanted to find out who took them, they could."

"But Drake knows what I can do. And if he does, I bet he's told people. At least those higher up in the PIB."

"Yes, well, there's not much we can do about it, but we're trying."

I swallowed. There was something he wasn't telling me. "But why now? Why the panic?" Oh, and they were trying to undermine their boss. This couldn't end well.

He took a deep breath, and his brow creased. "You can't repeat this to anyone, not even Mill, and not William. Beren knows, but best not to talk about it at all, in case somewitch overhears. Ma'am and I both believe the agency has been compromised. We can't prove it, but neither of us trusts Drake, and it's hard to say who he's planted to spy internally. Let's just say Dana's return is interesting, considering they're trying to cut costs for our branch. She's one of the highest paid agents, and she was happy in New York, or so we've heard via the grapevine. Her returning makes no sense."

Melancholy settled in between my ribs, making it hard to breathe. "But what about for Will? Maybe she really loves him and would do anything to get him back."

His eyes hardened. "I would give anything to see my friend happy, and she's not the person to do that. She's not here for him, and if he lets her in, she'll destroy him all over again. But I don't think he's that forgiving. She's been doing her best to seduce him, and so far, he's resisted. Whether he's a decoy to hide her true reason for being here or he's a fun way for her to pass the time while she's here, I can't say. But whatever the reason, it's not because she loves him. I don't even know if that woman is capable of that emotion."

Wow, that was harsh, and from someone who hadn't even dated her and had their heart broken. Hang on. "You haven't dated her, have you?"

"What? No! But I've seen her put my best friend through hell. No one with a functioning heart would do the things she's done."

Nevertheless, love made people do stupid things—like take witches back. There must be more to the story than what Millicent told me earlier. I was pretty sure James wouldn't tell me, so I didn't bother asking. "So what happens now? Am I in more danger? And does Drake know Millicent's pregnant?"

"No, he doesn't, and we're working on ways to keep the pregnancy a secret. I don't know that you're in any more danger than you were yesterday, but tomorrow morning, you're going to come to my place. I've set up the garage out back—we're going to practice physical self-defence and attack spells. Having a combination of both should help keep you safe. We should've started with this stuff earlier, but I'm ashamed to say we underestimated the risks, especially with that crazed brother after you."

"Yeah, but we have an alarm spell now."

"But what if he's been studying where you go on your daily runs? He could go on your route and set coordinates so he can pop there at any time. He probably wouldn't give a crap if someone saw him appear. He's beyond that."

Great. Way to scare me. Now I couldn't even run without looking over my shoulder? "Fine. But, just so you know, this all totally sucks. And what are you going to do about Drake?"

"Don't worry, Lily. We'll figure it out, but just leave that to Angelica and me. We have some digging to do first, find out who he's told. I'll let you know when it's sorted."

"Okay. Um, I've been reading Mum's diaries, and I wanted to take some pictures at Churchill's garden. Apparently Mum and Dad visited there on their last trip. And do you know if Mum was still working for the Bureau when she went missing?"

He looked down at his lap. When his eyes met mine, they were sad, remorseful. "She was. Sorry I didn't tell you before. It was supposed to be a secret, but I don't see the harm in you knowing since you're trying to figure out what happened."

I wrinkled my forehead so hard, a headache started. "Why didn't you tell me? That's not such a big secret."

"I didn't want you to question whether you knew our parents. You've had so many shocks since your birthday, and I didn't think it mattered. And I didn't want you to distrust the PIB. I love my job, and I was actually hoping you'd come work with me full-time."

I shook my head. "I already said no, and with everything you've just told me, it's even more of a no."

"I know. And you're right... for now. Anyway, I have to get going before Drake wonders where I am. I'll see you tomorrow at nine. Oh, and we'll talk about your trip to Churchill's tomorrow."

Well, that was better than being told no, it's too dangerous. We stood and hugged. "See you tomorrow, big bro."

"Bye, Lily." He turned and disappeared, leaving me with more than a seed of worry buried in my stomach. He still wasn't telling me everything, and in this case, what I didn't know would probably kill me. It wasn't the first time I'd wished my parents were here to talk to, to bounce things off. But they weren't.

I couldn't help but wonder what the hell was coming next.

CHAPTER 12

T he next morning, as I was about to travel to James's place, my phone rang. It was a number I didn't recognise. I almost didn't answer it, then figured it might be Patrick. "Hello?"

"Hello, Lily? It's Patrick."

"Oh, hey. How's it going?"

"Good. I can't really chat now, but I wanted to know if you were free this afternoon for a coffee? I'd really like to see you again."

Oh, wow, that was nice, and so soon. We'd only caught up yesterday. I couldn't help but wonder if he meant it, or if he needed information—maybe he was double undercover, criminal style. I wasn't judging though. Pot… kettle. "Yeah, sure. I'm about to go out, but I can meet you this afternoon. Where and what time?"

"Four at the same place as last time."

"Sounds good. See you then."

"Bye, Lily. Can't wait to see you."

I smiled, even though he couldn't see it. My ego couldn't help being pleased that he was so eager to see me, and it told my logical brain to shut up and take a number. I'd deal with any negative thoughts later.

I stepped out into James's reception room. It wasn't large, but it was bursting with character. A 1930s timber bureau sat against one wall, a blue-and-white vase filled with mauve hydrangeas on the top. The flagstone floor was varying shades of grey. The timber door was painted peacock blue, and a small window let in the morning light. This would actually make a cute reading room—it was wasted as a witchy reception room.

I knocked on the door. James answered. "Morning, sis." He gave me a quick hug, then led me through to the kitchen. "Have you had breakfast?"

"Yes. Coffee. Is Mill at work?"

"She left ten minutes ago. And coffee is not a proper breakfast. Mum would be horrified."

As sad as not having her here was, I smiled. She used to be a proponent of "breakfast is the most important meal of the day." She'd often cook us bacon and eggs, pancakes, or porridge. "So, are you going to make pancakes?"

"I can if you like."

"Nah. As good as it sounds, I'll vomit if you're going to have me working out this morning."

"At least have some toast."

"Okay. One piece with butter and strawberry jam."

He held his hand palm up. A plate holding a piece of toast appeared. "Just as you like it: lightly browned, not too dark."

I grinned. "You remembered!" I took the plate and ate standing. When I'd finished, there was a knock on the reception-room door. I looked at him. "Are you expecting anyone?"

"Yes. Someone to help with training. Just a sec." He left to unlock the door. Was it going to be some specialist combat agent?

I heard him before I saw him, and my heart raced. Gah! Damn traitor, my brother. Had Millicent been in his ear, or had he done this without an ulterior motive except my training?

I quickly put my plate in the dishwasher and wiped my mouth with my hand, just in case there were crumbs or jam or something.

They came through the door. "Morning," I said, doing my best "I'm so casual" impersonation.

"Morning, Lily. Ready to train?" William was all business, but God, did he look good in his running shorts and black T-shirt. I was wearing my long black running tights and a red tracksuit jacket over a black T, but he didn't even look twice or wait for an answer. He just kept on walking, straight out the back door. James shrugged and motioned me to follow, while he trotted along behind me.

James's shed was the size of a two-car garage. It was equipped with heating and ugly grey carpet squares. At least the walls and ceilings had plasterboard linings and downlights, so it wasn't super horrible. A punching bag hung from the ceiling to one side, and there was the obligatory weights bench with different sized weights stacked on steel holders next to the wall. The middle of the room was left open, probably for sparring or whatever the hell we were about to do.

I started by stretching while James and William conversed quietly in one corner. After five minutes, James said, "Okay. Let's start."

The guys walked to the middle of the room and faced each other. I stood to the side and watched. William grabbed James's wrist and said, "The first few moves are defensive. If someone grabs you, there are things you can do to release yourself and run. And I know you're good at running, so this will serve you well." He smiled.

James circled his arm all the way around in a wide arc to the side as he stepped in the same direction, dislodging Will's hand. "Now you try."

Hmm, that looked easy, but I bet I was going to stuff it up. I stood in front of William and looked up into his blue-grey eyes. Crap. My heart was racing, and some invisible force was pulling me to him, but I stood my ground. *Down, hormones. We don't like him. Got it?*

He reached out and grabbed my left wrist with his right hand. I tried to remember exactly what James had done. I pushed my arm out to the left and stepped while making a massive circle with my arm. And hey, it worked! "I did it!"

William gave a small smile, but James was grinning. "Nice work. Now, do it again, but add in a bit of force at the end, kind of flick your arm down hard, then get ready to run." I did as he asked, and we practiced it on both sides at least ten times.

They showed me two other moves for when someone grabs your wrist, and we practiced those before moving onto getting out of a chokehold when someone has both hands around your neck. I really could have used this with stupid Snezana—the crazy witch who kidnapped my brother.

After we'd done all that, I checked my watch. 9:45. We'd been at this for forty-five minutes. I hoped I didn't forget anything. I'd probably have to practice every day. "Can I come and practice with you, James, to make sure I don't forget?"

"Yeah, sure, plus I can teach you some other stuff. Why don't we make this a permanent thing, but we'll do 7:30. Angelica's giving me time off for this, but she won't be able to next time. I have to be at work by 9:00 am at the latest, and that's if we don't have something special going on."

"Yep, that works for me."

"Speaking of which, I have to get going. William can teach you the magic part of today's lesson by himself. He's the expert at that anyway."

My mouth dropped open. Oh, hell no! That was so unfair. How was I supposed to control my hormones when we were in a room by ourselves, touching each other? It was likely to end in me misreading some signal of his, trying to kiss him, then him awkwardly telling me to get off him. "You can't leave."

"I have to. What's wrong? You're not scared of Will, are you? He's just a big teddy bear." James smirked.

"Of course I'm not scared of him." At least not how he thought. "Okay, well how long will this part take?"

Will folded his arms. "About twenty minutes. But if you can't handle it, we can do it another time."

"What? I can handle anything you throw at me." I narrowed my eyes and put my hands on my hips. He shook his head and smirked.

"Okay, I'm out of here. Don't hurt my sister, dude." James threw Will a meaningful look.

"She's safe with me, unless she hurts herself." He snorted.

James grinned. "Fair enough. See you both later." He stepped through a doorway and vanished.

And then there were two.

Crap.

He pinned me with his gaze, although from his point of view, he was probably just plain old looking at me with no ulterior motive than to get this lesson over and done with. Fine. I needed to get with my program, which was to ditch this stupid crush. I gave a nod. "Right. I'm ready."

"Good. So, firstly, when fighting with magic, you need to be aware of what protections your opponent has. There are many different protection spells, and they all do different things. You're going to have to learn what they all are so you can recognise them, how to cast them, and how to defeat them. Here." He held his hands out, palms up, and a red hardcover book, about the size of a large dictionary, appeared in them. He handed the book to me. Whoa, it was heavy.

Ashford's Contemporary Spell Compendium, Fifth Ed. Wow. This was way bigger than the beginner book of spells I had. It seemed quite a jump going from kindergarten (in witch years) to university. "Um, am I allowed to have this?"

He wrinkled his brow, and it made me realise that all morning, he'd had a smooth brow. Hmm, maybe Piranha was actually making him happy. I sighed.

"Of course you're allowed to have it. Why wouldn't you be?"

"Ma'am. I'm not supposed to perform spells—well, anything above infant level—without an experienced witch present."

"What am I?"

"Yes, but I'm guessing I get to keep it when we finish today, so I can learn the stuff I need to." At least I hoped I would get to keep it. Excitement built through my fingers and toes, but I contained any jumping around. I grinned instead.

Will grinned too. "Yes, you can keep it. I expect you to learn that whole book from front to back, but don't perform any spells unless you're with an adult." He snorted.

I shook my head. "You are such an ass. Just you wait till I know what I'm doing."

His eyes darkened, and his voice was almost a growl. "Is that a threat, Lily?"

My heart raced, and my stomach went fluttery. I swallowed. I was pretty sure he was flirting with me, but why, when he had Dana Piranha trying to sink her lethal teeth into him? Maybe I'd flirted with him first, and he was just having a bit of fun? *You are not doing this now, Lily. Stop*! "Not a threat. More a warning. Now, what do I need to know?"

He blinked, all the heat leaving his gaze. Then he slow-nodded and refocused. "As you've been told, no doubt, there are spell protections that can cause a spell to bounce back to the caster, doing to them that which they tried to do to someone else."

I nodded. "But what if you both have the spell to bounce back spells? Does it keep bouncing between you like a pinball machine?" I snorted.

"No. You can't protect yourself from your own spell. Your magic knows you and will find a way in."

"If my magic knows me, shouldn't it not want to hurt me? Shouldn't it make allowances for my mistakes?"

"Unfortunately, no. Magic is partly you and partly the source, or universe, as you like to think of it." He smiled. "We're getting off track. The point of what I'm trying to say is that when a person has a defence or protection spell in place, you should be able to see it with your third eye."

"So, if you're in aura-seeing mode, you can see the spell?"

"Yes. Each spell will be a golden symbol, kind of like hieroglyphics. You'll have to learn what each spell looks like and memorise it."

My mouth dropped open, and my brain froze. Not possible. Maybe I could just lock myself inside Angelica's house and never leave again because that would be more effective than memorising all that other stuff. Why did being a witch require a good memory?

"Hey, don't worry. You'll be fine. Just learn one a day. There may even be a spell to help you remember." He winked.

"Well, why didn't you say something before?"

"The spell helps you remember for a week or two, but then you have to remember yourself, or redo the spell as you look at the symbols. But the more you look at them, the more likely you'll remember them anyway. Until you get used to them, it's a good idea to do the spell if you know you're going out, just to be safe. But eventually, you'll recognise them on sight. Like how you recognise business logos."

"They're not as complicated as these." He was crazy if he thought this was going to be easy. This was *me* we were talking about. But now, I just wanted to get this over and done with, see if I was capable or not. I wasn't into loads of suspense. "Can we get started?"

"Okay. Shut your eyes, draw some power, and focus on the space between your eyes—your third eye."

I did as he said and felt the power heating the spot at the top of the bridge of my nose. I opened my eyes and gasped. William's golden aura was so bright and crisp, so much shinier than other people's auras—not that I'd seen many. And there was heat radiating from it. I stepped close enough to touch him, and I raised my hands, facing my palms towards him to just feel his heat.

His voice was so quiet that I almost didn't hear him. "What are you doing, Lily?"

"I can feel warmth radiating from you. Is that the power, or is that you?" When I met his gaze, he was staring at me, his mouth slightly open. He grabbed one of my wrists, firmly but not enough to hurt. Energy zapped down my arm, leaving tingles in its wake. My breathing came faster. I had no other name for this other than super-duper attraction. Dangerous. The type of attraction that got hearts broken and, if this heat was anything to go by, eyebrows singed.

I used the move James had shown me earlier. Stepping away, I circled my arm and flicked my wrist out of his grip. He blinked and shook his head. "You shouldn't be able to feel anything. Can you do that with other people?"

"I... I don't know."

He ran a hand through his dark hair. "This isn't going to work, Lily. You're too new at this. I'll speak to Angelica, and she can take over. I'm sorry."

What the hell? He already knew I didn't know anything. What a lame excuse. "Are you bailing on me?" Our "moment" had sent him running, apparently. Maybe he felt guilty since he was supposed to be patching things up with chompy witch.

"I'm not equipped to deal with your magic, Lily."

Was he implying this wasn't something between us but that I had another talent? I shook my head. I was pretty sure this had never happened with anyone else, but I'd have to test my theory on Angelica to make sure. "Don't worry, Will. You're off the hook. Thanks for your time so far. Besides, I have a date this afternoon, so now I have time to get ready properly."

His eyes widened slightly. Ha. I hoped he was irritated or even pissed off. Although that was probably too much to wish for. Argh, I was losing the plot. I didn't have time for this. I had to learn to protect myself, and quickly. I was sick of being vulnerable… in every sense of the word.

I turned and made a doorway. It was time to rely on someone I could trust.

Myself.

CHAPTER 13

I was going to meet Patrick at the café, but he'd insisted on picking me up, and he even drove normally. Maybe there was hope for him yet. He certainly looked dapper in black jeans and a white T-shirt that wasn't crazy tight, but showed off his fit physique. The V-neck revealed that he wasn't hairy, which was awesome. Everyone liked different stuff, and I wasn't into super hairy. Which was fine because we couldn't all compete for the same men, now, could we?

He picked a table in the corner—nice and cosy. He ordered the pea-and-ham soup, and this time, I ordered a hot chocolate and a toasted cheese and tomato sandwich.

He took his black sunglasses off and tucked one sunglass's plastic arm over the V of his T-shirt, letting them hang. "So, what did you get up to this morning?"

"Just a workout at home. Nothing exciting. What about you?"

His expression turned serious. "We had a work meeting. Mrs Valentine's still missing, and we were deciding whether to have a special tribute show in the next few weeks or wait. We were all hoping she'd have turned up by now, but it's looking worse and worse the longer it goes on." His shoulders sagged, and he looked genuinely sad.

"Does anyone know what could have happened to her?" How had I gotten so lucky that he'd brought the subject up without my prompting?

He shook his head. "Nope. Her brother came in late yesterday, asking questions. He seems to think one of the art society members did something to her for the inheritance, but that's crazy. Why would we? We don't benefit personally —it's the people of Westerham and Kent who would get the most benefit."

"Oh, how so?"

The waitress arrived with our food and drinks. I sipped my hot chocolate—which was definitely yummier than their coffee had been— and Patrick had a sip of his orange juice before he answered. I mini-scrunched my face—I couldn't help it. Who has orange juice and soup at the same time? I bet he even drank orange juice after he brushed his teeth. Weirdo.

"Well, the society plans to move to bigger premises and hold more shows and competitions—they're all free for visitors, so not only do the residents win, but it attracts visitors to the area, and we support local artists at the same time.

We can also afford to run a couple of free art lessons per week for pensioners and students."

"That sounds good." This conversation was okay, but it wasn't getting me any really juicy information. I stared into his eyes, making sure I looked as earnest as possible. I clung to the fact that I was asking because I wanted to find her—she was a nice lady, and Knight needed justice too. "Do you have any idea what could have happened to her? I mean, I can't believe anyone would want to hurt her."

He looked around the café, as if checking for eavesdroppers. He leaned forward and whispered, "Her brother was more than annoyed that we inherited most of her estate—not that we'll be getting anything soon. No body means a longer waiting time for probate. Don't get me wrong—I hope they find her alive somewhere. Maybe she was so upset, she became confused and wandered off." He must have seen my sceptical expression because he quickly added, "It's happened before, you know."

"Hmm, maybe. How do you know the art society is getting an inheritance from her?"

"She told us. She decided about six months ago. Ida's always been one of our biggest supporters, including selling her artwork exclusively through us." I could swear he sat up straighter and puffed his chest out. I wasn't in art circles, but was that such a big deal with a lesser-known artist? Who knew?

"So, if something awful has happened to her, you won't get any more artwork to sell. Which is bad, I'm assuming."

He nodded. "Anyway, let's talk of happier things. Do you play tennis?"

I almost suffered whiplash from the change of subject. "Ah, I had some lessons when I was a kid, but I haven't played for a few years. Do you play?"

"Yes. I was school champion two years in a row. My parents and I play every Monday night. It's doubles, so nothing too strenuous, and my mother isn't very good, bless her heart. We normally have another couple who play with us, but they're on holidays next week. Would you like to attend this coming Monday? I could pick you up at quarter to six. We play for two hours, not even five minutes from here."

Surprisingly, that sounded like fun. A bit of exercise outdoors would be nice. "I'd love to, but I don't have a racquet."

He smiled. "I'll lend you one. I have several." Yes, he was being nice, but why did he come across as so pompous? It had to be more than the posh accent. I mean, who brags about having several tennis racquets? Maybe I was being harsh because the PIB were investigating him and his colleagues. From what Patrick said, though, there didn't seem like much reason for them to need the inheritance, unless the art society was struggling financially. I'd have to ask Angelica later.

We finished lunch, and he dropped me home.

I spent the rest of the afternoon looking through the book Will had given me. The most effective protection spell that covered pretty much everything was the return-to-sender spell, but it used the most power when one was attacked. Because it wasn't specific to, say, a lightning-bolt spell, it used more magic to pull together the correct way to deflect each different spell. It might only survive three or four attacks before you had to run, providing you still had the energy. The more specific the spell, the less power it used. But the problem was, if you had protection in place for four specific spells, your opponent could see which spells they were by looking at your aura. They could then create a spell you weren't ready for. The only answer to that would be a quick blocking spell. That would take hours and hours and hours of practice to be able to do on a whim.

I was tired just reading about it all. Because I wasn't a quitter, I managed to memorise the blocking spell—I'd just have to practice using it. I figured that was the most efficient use of my time, and I'd read over the return-to-sender spell and memorised what it looked like, just in case someone else had it in place. Something nagged at me, though. And then I realised an important point. Very important. If I learned an attack spell—like lightning bolt—I would need to put that protection spell on myself, in case I needed to use the spell against someone with a return-to-sender spell. Providing I was just as strong at magic as they were, I could withstand it far more times than they could if I was specifically protected against that spell and they only had general protection. Hmm, I was cleverer than I thought. I laughed.

"What are you laughing at, dear?" Angelica entered the sitting room. I hadn't even heard her come home because I'd been so wrapped up in my brilliance.

"Just musing about how awesome I am." I grinned. "I've been reading through this." I held up the book.

"Ah, yes. William told me he gave you that. Good. It's time you learned more taxing spells. I think we should practice now. How many spell symbols did you memorise?"

"I wouldn't say memorise, exactly, but I think I could recognise three or four symbols, but I could be wrong, because if there are other similar ones, I might mistake them for the ones I know."

"Which one would you like to start with?"

"The main one—return-to-sender."

"Okay. I'm going to cast a protection spell, and you tell me if it's return-to-sender." Her lips barely moved, and then she raised her arms. "Now, pretend I'm about to cast a spell, and read my aura quickly."

I didn't waste time agreeing; instead, I tapped into the ever-running river of power and concentrated my thoughts to my third eye while I looked at Ma'am. A golden symbol shone brighter than her aura, although with all the light and similar colour, it wasn't easy to see. "I don't think that's it. It's hard to tell, but it looks like there's an extra line cutting across the middle."

Ma'am smiled. "Very good, Lily. Or was that luck?"

"I'm pretty sure it was my awesomeness." I rubbed my fingernails of one hand on the top of my shirt, then blew on them and snorted.

"Beginner's luck, maybe? Are you ready for the next one?"

"Just a moment." I needed to change the colour of the

symbol because it would be clearer. Black would probably work, but now I had to come up with some stupid rhyme. I bit my lip and thought.

"This century, dear."

"Okay. Go." I mumbled, "The golden protection symbols are hard to see; make them black and easy to read."

Ma'am's aura glowed golden around her, maybe a handspan thick. Embedded in the incandescence directly above her head was a black symbol. And that was the one. I was sure about it, but then I was scared it wasn't the right one because whenever I'd been sure at school, that was the time I was wrong, as if I expected this to be a "trick question." "That's return-to-sender."

"Are you sure?"

"Ah, will something bad happen to me if I'm wrong?" My mouth went dry. Maybe she'd hurt me a little bit—an electric shot to the bottom?

"Not this time, but if I were an enemy..." She raised her brows.

"Point taken. But I stand by my answer." A wrong decision was better than no decision; at least that's how I'd always lived my life. Act now, pay later.

Her expression remained neutral when she spoke. "You're correct. Good work, Lily."

I grinned and fist pumped the air. "Yes!" So her praise wasn't super enthusiastic, but compared to usual, it was a resounding endorsement.

Ma'am shook her head, but I saw the miniscule lip twitch. "Okay, now for the next one."

We repeated the process for an hour, and I made two mistakes out of dozens of tries. Not bad, if I did say so myself. By the time we finished, I was drained of energy and starving. Ma'am looked at her watch. "Time for dinner. Would you please call Olivia down?"

"Yes, Ma'am. And thanks for working with me."

"It's all part of my job. Sorry I haven't had time to help you much lately. Just some advice: learn the electric shock spell and other subtle ones. It's not good if you find yourself in public to call down lightning bolts. You'll create a ridiculous amount of memory wiping for my team. And if a witch causes too much trouble, they can be fined, even jailed. Our security is very important, dear. Our lives could be very different if the public found out who we really are and what we can do. Fear is a motivator for horrific things, Lily. So always put the safety of the witch community before your own."

"Oh. Okay. I'll make sure to be careful." I pouted. All those exciting spells I'd been itching to do were pretty much forbidden, unless you were in an empty field or room. I would be lying if I said I wasn't disappointed I couldn't go zapping and smiting in the most obvious ways. I imagined it would have been very satisfying. A small electric shock to the posterior didn't have quite the same oomph, kind of like saying fudge instead of f—

"Lily, are you going to get Olivia? I'm sure she's just as hungry as you."

I shook the cobwebs from my head. I also remembered I hadn't tried to see if I felt warmth from Ma'am's aura.

Maybe I didn't really want to know. "Sorry. Going now." I hurried up to our floor and knocked on Olivia's door. Within five minutes, we were all sitting around the dining table in the kitchen, digging into a delicious dinner of lasagne and garlic bread, care of Ma'am's magic.

As much as I didn't want to, it was time to ask Ma'am's permission for my outings. Sweat slicked my palms. I hadn't felt this nervous about asking something for years. The last time was probably when I was twelve and asking my dad if I could go to the school disco. He'd been strict, and whenever I wanted to do anything, it was a big drama and usually ended in a "no" and me crying in my room for hours. Knowing now what they knew then, no wonder he'd wanted to keep me close to home. "Ma'am, I have a couple of outings I need your approval for."

She put her fork down. "And where and when are they?"

"I've been asked to play tennis with Patrick and his family on Monday night at..." Ah, crap. He hadn't said where exactly. "I'll get back to you on the where. It's apparently five minutes from here. The other thing is that I would like to visit Churchill's house and garden. That would be during the day. Maybe tomorrow or Thursday?"

"Monday night should be fine; just get me the location by Sunday so I can plan. Yes to Churchill's. However, I can't confirm the date. I was going to ask you something after dinner, but since we're almost finished... We need your unique skill to find out where Mrs Valentine went. I'm sending you and Millicent out on the road tomorrow morning. She's picking you up at seven. I'd like you to start outside Mrs Valentine's brother's place, but you're not to put yourself or Millicent in any danger. I'll have two other agents following, so don't be too obvious about taking photos. Stay in the car when you take them, if it's at all possible."

"I can do that. I'd take them with my phone to be even more discreet, but the zoom and photo quality isn't good enough. Could I hide what I'm doing by casting a spell to make the windows look dark from the outside without making it darker from inside looking out?"

"Yes, you could. But maybe ask Millicent to do it. It will be easier for her. And don't tell anyone else. We won't have a formal PIB meeting once you have the results. We'll have a get-together at James's, but Millicent will let you know. It all depends on what you find tomorrow, and if your search leads you to Brighton, you'll have a long day ahead. I've left other instructions with Millicent, and she's in charge, Lily, so you do whatever she says. Understood?"

I nodded and resisted the urge to wriggle. The thrum of excitement built inside at the thought of finally finding out where Mrs Valentine had gone. "Yes, Ma'am."

She raised a brow. "No deviations. I mean it. You don't want to endanger her or the baby, do you?"

"Of course not!" I knew I deserved her scepticism after the whole Paris car crash incident, but I'd promised I'd learned my lesson. Okay, so going "undercover" was a bit risky, but not much, and I was keeping her up to date on where I was and when.

She gave me a stern glare; then her expression relaxed

to her usual poker face. "So, why do you want to visit Churchill's?"

Oh, she was good, attacking me with that when I wasn't prepared. I practiced my poker face. I was an amateur, but everyone had to start somewhere, right? "I've been living here for ages, and it's silly that I haven't visited the most famous former inhabitant's home. It was probably one of the first things I should have done." I shrugged. I could have told her the truth—that it had to do with Mum's diary, but bringing it up would only upset her, and my theory that I might find out something about their disappearance by going there was only that—a hunch.

"I'd love to go with you, Lily. If you'd like some company." Olivia smiled. Either she was backing me up because she suspected there was a more important reason I didn't want to share or she just had really good timing.

I grinned. "That would be great. I'll let you know the date when I know."

She laughed. We both looked at Angelica. "Yes, ladies. I'll give you an appropriate date once we know where Mrs Valentine's investigation is going. I have so much happening that I don't want to rush things and end up putting anyone in danger. One thing at a time, please." She was starting to sound like my brother.

I nodded. "Yes, Ma'am."

Everyone had finished eating, and Angelica magicked the food and mess away. I yawned, then bade Angelica and Olivia goodnight. Today had been exhausting, and I had an early start the next morning. The sooner I went to sleep, the sooner tomorrow would come, and we'd be that much closer to finding Mrs Valentine.

I made sure all my camera equipment was ready to go before I hopped into bed. I didn't want anything slowing us down.

As I slid into bed, the cold breath of foreboding feathered the back of my neck. I shuddered. Why couldn't I get a kiss goodnight instead, like a normal person?

Oh, that's right: I was far from normal.

CHAPTER 14

What good was magic if you couldn't change the weather? Millicent and I sat in the car outside Mrs Valentine's brother's house. Rain pounded the car roof and bled rivulets down the windows. I turned to Millicent, who was wearing normal clothes today —we'd agreed it would make us look less conspicuous if we had to get out of the car. I could never understand how you could be a secret agent when you were so obviously dressed like one. Sharp black suits, white shirts, and black ties screamed secret service. "I don't think the visibility will affect what shows up in the past—unless it was raining and dark then as well. At least there's fewer people stopping to notice what we're doing."

"True."

I scrunched my forehead. Gah, what if I had to get out

and my camera got drenched? "Do you have a spell to fix my camera if it gets ruined?"

She tilted her head and looked at me. "Yes, but why wouldn't I just protect it from getting wet in the first place?"

"Der me. Would you be able to?" But then something niggled at me. "What if your magic stops mine from working?"

She touched a fingertip to her nose, thinking. "Oh, wow, you could have something there. I don't actually know. This is a pretty unique circumstance. It's probably best not to mess with that. I can always fix it later if there's a problem, and that's not a constant spell, so it shouldn't interfere with anything."

"Thanks. We'd best do it that way then."

We'd pulled over onto the grass verge across the road and up a little bit from Ida's brother's. As quaint as the English countryside was with its narrow lanes and roads, it left little room for parking, which was kind of annoying. I was going to have to get out of the car to get a clear shot of the street in every direction. I had my raincoat on, and I'd used a small clear plastic sandwich bag to cover my camera while leaving the lens part clear, but the rain was coming down hard, and it was likely to wet my baby. Those umbrellas you wear on your head that I laughed at when the ad came along on Facebook would actually have come in handy today. That would teach me to laugh at other people's inventions, no matter how stupid they seemed.

I drained the last of my takeaway coffee and put it back in the cup holder. Then I turned on my camera and dropped the lens cover into my camera bag at my feet. "I'm going out," I said in a this-is-getting-serious voice. It was meant to sound like when they say, "I'm going in," in the movies, but Millicent looked at me like, yeah, I know. Why did no one get my jokes? I snorted anyway, both at my humour and the fact that I was the only one who found me funny.

I pulled my raincoat hood up, jumped out of the car, and slammed the door, swiftly placing the camera to my face. "Show me Ida Valentine's car last time she was here." A yellow Mini appeared, and it wasn't raining. Yes! A swarm of dizziness circled my head as relief loosened my shoulder and neck muscles.

It was evening in the shot and not all the way dark yet. The car was in the middle of the road, about fifty metres away, facing in the opposite direction, so she must have been driving. I snapped a few shots and ran along the grass towards the car. My raincoat rubbed against my hair as I moved, rustling loudly, as if I were in another world. Fat droplets pitter-pattered on my head—unfortunately, it wasn't as comforting as listening to that same sound when you were inside and dry.

Just before I ran into the middle of the road, I remembered I was in "now" time. Crap. I stopped, my foot on the edge where grass met bitumen, and glanced up the road. A car was metres away and closing fast. My blood pounded in my throat in time with my racing heart. Jesus, Lily. Way to kill yourself. The car whooshed past, sending up a spray of water.

I tried to shrink back into my raincoat while I took a few steadying breaths. This time, I looked both ways before I did anything. All clear. Idiot me. I went to the space in front of the yellow Mini and took some shots of Mrs Valentine's face, which was set into an exhausted, sad expression. I zoomed in, snapped a shot, then returned to the safety and shelter of Millicent's car.

"Did you almost step in front of that car?" Millicent sounded like the mother she was soon to be.

"Yes. I get caught up in what I'm doing, and I forget what I see through my lens isn't the here and now." I flicked my hood down so I could see properly, then grabbed a lens-cleaning cloth and wiped the droplets off the glass before replacing the lens cap. "I know I'm stupid. I don't need reminding."

She blew out a breath, and her expression softened. "It's okay. I just... God, Lily, if anything happened to you, we'd all be devastated. Just remember to be careful, okay?"

"Thanks. I'll do my best to remember. I won't get offended if you remind me every now and then." I gave her a small smile.

She grinned. "Okay, so where to now?"

"She was heading the other way, west. What's in that direction?"

"Brighton, among other places."

Millicent drove until the road continued straight or you could make a left turn. She pulled over, and this time, I stayed in the car to take the photos. I focussed on the road in front of us. "Show me the last time Ida Valentine drove through here. Show me her car." The yellow Mini appeared, still heading straight. I lowered the camera. "Okay, Mill. Keep straight."

Every time we came to a potential turnoff, she pulled over, and I snapped. It was like walking a dog that had to mark every freaking tree. Whoever was following us—and there were sure to be at least one group of people, if not more at this point—was probably wondering what the hell we were doing. I snorted.

Millicent glanced at me as she drove. "Dare I ask?"

"We're the Pied Pipers of pulling over. I bet there are a lot of confused stalkers back there somewhere."

She laughed. "Too true."

We continued until we came to a main left turn that headed south… to Brighton. What was normally about a one-hour drive turned into an hour and twenty minutes— both because of the terrible weather and us pulling over every now and then.

Our journey finally ended around the corner from The Old Ship Hotel, which was opposite Brighton Beach. Many of the buildings looked to be from the 1800s to early 1900s and were brick, painted light shades—white, pink, yellow. Many of the structures had bay windows. I wondered if they had window seats, where the occupants could sit and read, glance out at the water every so often. I sighed. Everything was so damn quaint in this country. Apart from all the drama I'd been part of, I was glad I was here.

A gull wheeled overhead, its cry melancholy. It set off a yearning inside me to sit in one of those windows and soak up the heavy greyness and be one with the place, watch storms advance across the sea, bringing salt-tainted gales that frothed the top of the slate-grey water, and to observe life unfolding in its streets. I could totally understand why this was one of Mrs Valentine's favourite places.

From here, we could follow her trail on foot, but it was going to be rather uncomfortable. I turned to Millicent. "Are you sure you don't know any rain, rain, go away spells?"

She laughed. "If only."

"Or a make-it-rain spell. I'd totally cast one on Dana Piranha, and it could follow her around raining on her all day, like in the cartoons." I wiggled my fingers and evil laughed. I was totally going to work on that tonight.

"Remind me never to become your enemy." She grinned.

"Ha, not a chance. You're one of the good ones." I smiled. "Can we have a toilet break first?" I'd been drinking water as well as the coffee I'd finished ages ago, and I was busting.

"Yes, sure. Since no one can see in here, I think it's safe to pop into the local public toilet. Here are the coordinates." Golden numbers appeared in my mind, and I started. Sheesh, magic was so shocking. So much of it happened suddenly and took me off guard. I'd get used to it eventually, right?

We popped away, did what we had to, and returned. The bucketing rain had slowed to drizzle, but I still wasn't looking forward to wandering around in it. I grabbed my camera, then turned to Millicent and blinked. She was wearing a yellow raincoat she hadn't been in earlier, and she held a long, black umbrella. When was I going to stop being surprised and start using this witchy stuff myself? Was it this hard for every witch to get used to? I was only just getting onboard with protecting my thoughts every morning.

"I've got an extra big umbrella, so I can stop you from getting wet too." She smiled.

"Thanks, Mill. You are so thoughtful."

"I try." She got out of the car.

I pulled my hood up and stepped out. The tang of brine filled my nose, the faint taste of salt invading my mouth. I turned my camera on, then went to point it towards where Mrs Valentine's Mini had been parked, about fifty metres up the street. My mouth dropped open. "Millicent?"

"Yes." She opened her umbrella, stood close to me, and placed it over our heads.

"Do you see that yellow Mini over there?"

"Yes. Oh… Is that?" Excitement laced her tone.

"I think so. Come on." We hurried along the footpath to the car. My heart beat faster. "That's it, Mill. That's her number plate."

Millicent handed me the umbrella, then bent to look in the windows, careful not to touch anything. She stood straight again. "I'm calling Angelica."

"Wait! Let me take some photos first, to see where she went. We're trying to hide my talent, and if there are agents all over the place, it will be harder to do what I have to."

She hesitated, the phone already in her hand.

"Plus, I might find more clues, so then you can tell her

everything at once. It's just an extra ten or twenty minutes. Once we follow Mrs Valentine's path out of this street, I can take photos without everyone seeing." I bit my lip. I knew in my gut this was important. We'd come so close to finding her, and I didn't want anything stopping us. And with the duck and piranha on the loose, who knew what their agendas were? I just didn't want to risk it. "Please?"

She looked at her phone and back up at me. "Okay, Lily. Your reasoning is sound, but I don't want to leave the vehicle, in case something happens, and it disappears."

"But it's here now. Unless Mrs Valentine gets in and drives it away, which would actually be quite helpful because then we can call this whole thing off, how is it going to disappear? Do you think it will get towed?"

"No. If the person who took her is keeping tabs on us, they might decide to make it disappear."

"Wouldn't they have to be pretty powerful to do that?"

"Yes, but there are many powerful witches out there, Lily. You of all people should know that by now, what with everything that's happened since you got here." She rubbed her tummy, which was a dead giveaway she was pregnant.

"Don't do that!"

"Do what?" She sounded annoyed.

"Rub your belly. It's a total tell that you're, you know…"

Her eyes widened. "Oh my God. You're right. I shouldn't be out in the field." She looked around. Great, now she was worried about the baby, and we still had to finish what we came here to do.

"I'll get this done quickly. Just stay here."

She nodded, and I stood back, to take a photo of the car and its surrounds. "Show me the last time Mrs Valentine was here."

She appeared in twilight, wearing the clothes she'd left our art class in. She only had a handbag, but if she was a witch, I guessed she could magic clothes to herself anywhere she wanted. She had obviously locked her car and was walking away from us, towards the beach. But hang on. Was that someone in her car? I went right up to her car and looked into the back seat through my lens. I sucked in a quick breath.

Henry.

He hadn't been in there before. He must have popped in as soon as she had gotten out. It didn't mean he had killed her, though. I would find out where Mrs Valentine went first, and then I would figure out what Henry had been up to.

I followed her down the street, where she turned left.

She walked down a little way, then entered The Old Ship Hotel.

"Show me the next time Mrs Valentine came out of the hotel." All I saw through my lens was the drizzling day and the people in real time hurrying to get where they were going and out of the rain.

Mrs Valentine had gone in but had never come out—at least not the conventional way. Now for part two. "Show me if Henry was here the same day as Mrs Valentine."

And there he was, entering the hotel. The time of day looked the same, and, in fact, if I looked at the pier, the same people were there, only further down. So he had gone in straight after her. "Show me the next time he came out."

Today's almost-empty, puddle-ridden footpath stared back at me.

Crap.

I ran back to Millicent, careful not to slip on the slick footpath, the cold air burning my lungs. It was time to call Angelica.

Unfortunately for Mrs Valentine, we were probably too late.

CHAPTER 15

M a'am arrived, dressed in formal **PIB** gear—which included a jet-black raincoat—with a handful of agents to search the car. She consulted with them for a few minutes, her manner brisk and purposeful, before coming to fill Millicent and me in. "We've put a no-notice spell on ourselves, and we'll shortly be placing the car in evidence. Interestingly, there was already a no-notice spell on the car. The magic signature matches the one on the painting."

Well, that was interesting. "So it could be her or Henry?"

"Yes." Ma'am's phone rang. She answered it. "Yes. Okay… Fine… Right. Okay." She hung up. Well, that was insightful. "You ladies, come with me. We're going to the hotel, and I'll convince the clerk to show us her room. She may even have seen Henry, although, if he had a no-notice spell on himself, she likely won't remember. You can do your thing there, Lily. But I warn you: it could get ugly. Are you ready?"

"By ugly, do you mean blood and guts and dead body kind of ugly?" Because even though the sex I'd seen through my lens was icky, I could handle it. The other, however… I guessed I wouldn't know until I'd confronted it. Maybe I could pretend it was just a TV show or horror movie.

"Yes, dear."

"I'll deal. Let's just do this." Fear slithered in my belly, and my mouth went dry. I had to force myself to focus on my surroundings so I didn't freak out and run the other way. I mean, there was a good chance we weren't going to find anything gory, especially if we were dealing with a witch criminal. Who would make a mess in someone else's place where it could be found when you could whisk your victim away somewhere private and do it there? I shuddered.

As we rounded the corner and walked to the entrance of the hotel, the wind gusted, blowing rain into my face, chilling my cheeks and nose. I squinted into the distance. Even in this weather, people hurried along the pier that stretched quite a way out into the sea.

As we entered The Old Ship Motel and made our way to the reception area, Millicent said, "This is the oldest hotel in Brighton. Apparently part of it dates back to 1559." Wow, talk about history. Another reminder I'd done hardly any exploring while I'd been here. I would totally have to fix that when this case was done.

It was warm inside, so I pushed my hood off and wiped

my hand over my face, trying to get rid of some moisture. Millicent put her hand on my arm, slowing me, and whispered, "Let Ma'am take care of this. Let's go wait by the lift."

I let her guide me in that direction. I stopped a few metres from the lift and aimed my camera towards it. "Was Henry here the last time Mrs Valentine was?" And there he was, finger on the lift call button.

"Henry was in here too. Do you think they have security-camera footage we could ask for?"

"Yes, they should have." She pointed towards a camera in the ceiling corner. "It wasn't that long ago, and I know those systems can save lots of data."

"What if it's a system that only saves a couple of days' worth?"

"Let's not worry about that until it happens. And I'm sure magic could bring back what we need if it's not there." That was impressive.

I took a deep breath. If we couldn't find physical evidence, how would we explain to Drake how we got this far? "So, Mill, do you think Mrs Valentine is behind the spell on her car and artworks? I still don't see how Henry would benefit from her artwork selling well."

She pressed her lips together. "Maybe…"

"Well, if it wasn't Mrs Valentine who wanted to make her artwork more desirable, who else stood to gain, other than Henry?" I still hadn't given up on Henry just following her to make sure she was okay. Maybe that's all this was, and he'd lied to us because he didn't want to look guilty because he really wasn't.

"And that is the million-dollar question."

I jumped. Ma'am had snuck up behind us.

"I have a feeling we might just find out who it was once we get access to her room. She didn't check out when she was supposed to, and when they found her room vacant, they just billed her credit card. No one saw Henry, but I dug into her thoughts, and their security system keeps four weeks of recordings. If things pan out how I think, we'll say you ladies were here sightseeing, you lucked upon her car, and then me and my agents questioned local hotels until we found the one she stayed in. Then we'll be able to pull the security footage that proves they were here." She leant over and pushed the button to call the lift.

Okay, so we were getting somewhere. But Henry, a murderer? An idea was forming. "The other people, or should I say organisation, who stand to gain from her artwork sales is the art society. They get commission on her work, but if she's dead, don't they get the whole value?"

Millicent answered, "Yes, if they inherit her paintings. Did she leave any to anyone else?"

The lift doors opened, and Ma'am stepped through. "Apparently she left a handful to Henry."

Mill and I got in, and Ma'am pressed the button for the second floor.

"But is he desperate for her money? Wouldn't he want to keep the paintings for sentimental reasons?"

There were a couple of clunks as the lift ascended, then

reached our floor. The doors rolled open. Ma'am stepped out first and walked down the corridor, stopping at a door on the left. She unlocked it with the key, even though she probably didn't need it. I imagined getting the details from the clerk was just so we knew which room number it was, but it didn't hurt to get a key and confirm there was no one inside. Um… *had* she confirmed there was no one in there?

We walked in… to an empty room. Phew.

It was gorgeous. Eggshell-blue walls with a papered feature wall, which had white gulls on a blue background. A large sumptuous bed with grey velvet headboard sat against that wall, and a writing desk with a stripy upholstered armchair took up the opposite wall, and between them a clear path to a window with a sea view. This was a room I would love to stay in, except for the slimy sensation that smothered the back of my neck and scalp. I shuddered.

Ma'am regarded me. "Are you okay, Lily?"

"Yes, it's just… it feels weird, wrong somehow."

She nodded, a pleased albeit small smile curving her lips. "Your magic is coming along nicely. You're picking up on the magic and emotional energies that have recently happened here. Unfortunately, that means we're probably not going to like what we find."

I walked to the window and stared out at the water. The angry slosh of waves on the pebbled shore and the frenzied wind creating whitecaps on fields of gunmetal grey-green matched my mood. Nervous energy built inside me, and I wanted to run. Run all the way out of here, across the road to the pebbles, and keep on sprinting into the furious wind, feel the sting of cold rain on my face, be one with nature and the tempest outside. Instead, I was trapped in a room where it was likely the beginning of the end started for Mrs Valentine. I turned back to the room and fought against the energy that seemed to press in on me. My breathing increased, and dizziness hit.

Millicent grabbed my arm and took me to the bed. "Sit for a minute, Lily. It's okay. You're having a reaction to the lingering emotional energy. I know it's hard, but just slow your breathing, and you'll feel better."

I looked up at her. "Is this what you go through all the time?"

"Yes, but I'm used to it. It can be rather draining at times, but it's not all bad. A lot of the time, it's happy energy." She smiled. I hadn't realised how resilient she was. I hoped this wasn't going to turn into some special talent for me, because I didn't think I could handle taking everyone's emotions on board all day. Being an empath was draining.

I concentrated on breathing slowly until the dizziness disappeared. The longer I sat here, the longer I would be bombarded. That went for Millicent too. The quicker I got those photos, the better. I stood, pocketed my lens cap, and turned my camera on. I positioned myself at the door and brought the camera to my face. "Show me the last time Mrs Valentine was here with Henry."

I inhaled a sharp breath. My stomach flipped over, creating a tsunami that tried to escape via my mouth. My arm dropped, and I frantically looked for the door to the bathroom. I raced in, shoved the toilet lid up and loudly deposited my breakfast inside, careful to hold my camera out of splash range. The plop of chunks made me vomit more.

Oh, God, could I be any louder? I'd never been a quiet thrower upper. The shame.

I checked in with myself to make sure I'd finished. Yep, done. I straightened, flushed the toilet, rinsed my mouth out, and washed my face. Millicent handed me a towel and rubbed my back. "Are you okay?"

"No. Can't say I am. I didn't take any photos. Let's just get this done." I returned to the room and tried again with my lips pressed firmly together.

Click. Click. Click.

Mrs Valentine lay face down on the floor, the back of her skull bashed in, bits of blood and brain spattered around the room. Henry stood over her, hammer in hand, and his cold, vacant eyes as he stared down at her froze my blood. Nausea threatened again. *Just a few more, Lily. You can do this. Mrs Valentine and Knight need you to.*

I walked around Henry and his victim, getting shots from every angle of both them and the room. It almost sent me to the bathroom again, but I took close-ups. The echo of hammer striking bone reverberated in the silence. Was that a new thing or just my overactive imagination?

Finally, I lowered my camera and looked at Ma'am, tears gathering in my eyes. "Here." I handed her the camera. She didn't need any warning. My reaction had taken care of that.

I returned to the window as she and Millicent looked

through the pictures. I wrapped my arms around myself. How could someone do that to another person? And to someone they supposedly loved? I shook my head. Henry. Soft-spoken life-drawing old guy. How? It was apparent that monsters came in many forms.

Millicent stood next to me. "Are you okay?"

"Not really, but what can you do? What about you?"

"It never gets easier." We stared out the window while Ma'am spoke quietly on the phone.

"So, what now? Are we going to keep those photos from the PIB? I understand if this is more important than hiding my talent. It doesn't matter anyway: people will still be after me."

"Ma'am's calling a meeting with Beren and Will now. James is in Germany, working a case for Pemberton."

I bit my nail. "She's not going to call Dana, is she? There's something about her I don't trust."

"Oh, really?" Millicent raised a brow.

"No, not because of that." At least I was pretty sure it wasn't because of her and Will. "There's something more to her than everyone realises. If she knew my secret, I have no doubt I'd be in even more danger. I'm trusting my gut on this one."

"The same gut that had a tantrum earlier?" Millicent snickered.

"Yeah, yeah, make fun of the witch with the weak stomach."

"Don't worry, Lil. It's part of induction. We've all been

there. Trust me. Even James has chucked up on occasion, in the early days."

I hung my head. All those times I hadn't been there for my brother. All those lost years. If only he'd told me about this witch stuff earlier, I could have been here with him, helping. I raised my head and met Mill's gaze. "I'm glad you've been here for him. Thank you."

She took my hand and squeezed.

"Okay, ladies. Meeting at my place in thirty minutes. Give me your keys, Millicent, and I'll get one of the agents to drive your car back to headquarters. You've done enough running around for one day." She looked at Millicent's stomach.

"I'm fine, maybe a bit tired."

"As much as I'm sure you can handle the drive back, James would have my head if anything happened to you or the baby, so let's just humour him, okay?"

Millicent smiled. "If you insist."

I couldn't say I was disappointed at having to go home the magical way. Exhaustion had jumped on my back, demanding a ride, and it weighed the same as a professional rugby player.

Ma'am took my memory card and handed me the camera. She didn't have to say anything; I knew she'd give it back to me later. We'd done this so many times. "Can I go?"

"Yes, dear. I'll see you at the house soon. I'm just going to return the key."

"Are you going to look for any physical evidence first?"

"I have proof that Henry performed magic here, but I

have to send in the forensics team. I can't do that until we can order the video footage from that day. I will ask the staff if they remember him, but he wasn't here long, and, like I said, if he had his no-notice spell on... Still, there may be witches working here who could have seen past his spell. I'm going to get a couple of my agents to organise the interviews this afternoon. Don't worry, Lily. We're close to getting this guy. Now, go home before you collapse. You've used more magic than you can handle today. I imagine you have just enough energy left to travel. Now go."

Universe, please don't make all this be for nothing.

"Bye." I mumbled my doorway spell and left.

CHAPTER 16

I exited Angelica's reception room and looked longingly at the stairs. I would love to climb up them and go to bed, but not yet. I sighed. The only positive thing I could get from today—okay, well, two positives: we knew what had happened and who took her, and Knight would be with her, wherever that might be.

Was there life after death? That obviously wasn't the first time I'd asked myself that question, but I still didn't have an answer. Although, now that I knew about witches, life after death didn't seem as far a stretch as it used to. I guessed we could all hope.

I took my spot on one of the Chesterfields, and soon Millicent, Ma'am, Beren, and Will joined me. There was little chatter as everyone took their seats—Millicent on one side of me; Beren, the other. Ma'am and Will sat on the other sofa. With the guys and Ma'am dressed in their PIB gear, it felt as if we were at a funeral.

Ma'am called the meeting to order. "We have a bit to talk about this afternoon. First we'll start with Will's update on the interview with Maddison Archer."

I couldn't help asking. "But isn't that redundant now?"

Ma'am shook her head. "No, Lily. Her evidence could give us a reason to investigate Henry further, interview him again, and maybe get a confession if we're lucky, which would negate the need for your photos."

"Oh. Sorry." My face heated. I needed to think more before I spoke so I didn't look like a complete moron.

William mainly looked at Millicent and Beren while he spoke. It wasn't clear if he was avoiding eye contact with me because he thought I was irrelevant or if whatever sent him running the other day was still on his mind. "I interviewed Ms Archer at The Westerham Art Society gallery—she was in there setting up a showing today. She isn't a witch, but she reiterated her complaint that she always came second or third, and Mrs Valentine always won. She told me that once, Henry cornered her and warned her to stop her complaints. He didn't outright threaten her, but she was worried he'd do something to her paintings. I read her mind—she was genuinely sorry Mrs Valentine was missing, as she still wanted to beat her. It appears to have been a great ambition of hers. I also managed to put my hand on her shoulder and delve deeper. I found evidence that Henry tried to tamper with her mind, stop her from worrying about Mrs Valentine winning. Her subconscious has held onto it. It was a clumsy attempt, but it gives us a reason to question him again and demand he give us his magic signature." He looked at Angelica. "I would guarantee it will match the one on her car."

Angelica nodded. "Good. That along with the hotel confirmation Mrs Valentine had been there and the video footage should be enough to order him to provide his magic signature."

William stood. "I'll go grab Dana, and we'll visit Henry."

"Will." He finally looked at me, his eyes as dark and rugged as the ocean this afternoon. But his face was set in a mask of impatience.

"What, Lily? I have to go."

His short tone hurt, but this wasn't about my feelings, which he obviously didn't give a crap about. This was about my safety. "Just in case no one's told you: don't tell Dana about my talent. I'm in enough danger as it is."

He clenched his teeth, the muscle in his jaw bulging. "What are you implying, Lily?"

"Nothing much, except that it's my talent, and I don't want her knowing." I stood and faced him, my stare steady and unrelenting.

"She's right, Will. And don't worry, Lily; we've had this conversation." Ma'am placed a hand on his arm, and William backed down, his expression softening.

"Don't worry. I haven't told her."

"Good." I turned to Ma'am. "I'm going to have a lie-down. Can you please let me know if anything else happens?"

"Of course, dear. You're a big part of this investigation. I'll check in with you tonight."

"Thanks." I gave Millicent and Beren a quick hug, then left, not bothering to acknowledge Will. She was his girl-friend, and he obviously had no loyalty to me, even as a friend, if he was going to get his back up about a simple request. At least I could trust everyone else, but for now, William wasn't a friend anymore, and I'd have to assume anything he knew would be passed on to the piranha. Just went to show that you never really knew someone.

Mrs Valentine had found that truth out the hardest way there was.

CHAPTER 17

I dragged myself out of bed after a two-hour nap. Otherwise there was no way I would've slept that night. Olivia was around, so we ordered pizza, and I updated her on some of what I'd been up to. I knew I could trust her, and I was sure Ma'am wouldn't mind me telling her what we'd discovered—I had trusted her with the secret of my talent, which to me was more important. There wasn't anything she could do to derail our investigation into Mrs Valentine's murder at this point.

I'd just taken a bite of the cheese and anchovy pizza—and yes, lots of people hated anchovies, which meant I got it all to myself—when Ma'am strode into the kitchen. "Lily, I have some news."

Her poker face had slipped, and anger flashed in her eyes. Had I done something wrong? "What happened?"

"Will made an appointment to question Henry again, but when they got there, he'd gone. He's disappeared."

"Crap. How did he know?"

"He must have cast some kind of alarm spell on the hotel room, something to notify him if any witches were there looking around, or he may have even planted a camera. I'm not sure which, but however he found out we were onto him, the damage is done. He's gone."

Way to ruin a good pizza. I dropped my piece onto my plate, and Olivia frowned. She'd liked Mrs Valentine too, and I knew she was hoping we'd throw Henry in jail quickly.

"So now what?" I pushed my chair back. I didn't know what I could do to help, but whatever it was, I wanted to do it now.

"We've put an APB out throughout the UK and Europe. Both the normal police and the PIB are looking for him. The normal police don't need to know he's a witch, but they've been ordered to notify us before approaching him. As far as the average police officer knows, we're a government agency they have to answer to."

"Like the FBI are in the US?"

"Yes, like that. As I've told you before, there are some who know who we really are, and they help smooth the way for us."

"Are you going to search his house for her body? I mean, he had to have put it somewhere."

"There's a problem. He lived in a studio flat, and it appears he stayed with Mrs Valentine a lot."

"So he really was a leech." Olivia pursed her lips.

"Bastard." An image of Mrs Valentine lying on the hotel room floor with her brains oozing out of her head made me gag. "But why?"

"We may never know, Lily. Unless we catch him, and even then, he may not tell us." Ma'am rested her hand on my shoulder and squeezed. "We won't let up until he's caught. He can't have vanished. He's a witch, not a god."

"Are there gods?" Did she know?

She laughed. "I don't know, Lily. Do I look like I know everything?"

"Kind of. I really wouldn't be surprised." I smiled.

"Well, contrary to what everyone believes, I don't."

My phone dinged with a message. I unlocked it. Patrick.

Hi, Lily. Just confirming we're on for Monday night. Can't wait to have a hit with you, and for you to meet my parents. I'm sure they're going to love you. Patrick. He ended it with a smiley face and a heart. Didn't pick him for the romantic type, but that was nice.

Yes, of course. I'm looking forward to it. See you then. I just did the smiley face. I couldn't bring myself to send him a heart. Today had been crap, and my heart still stung from William's standoffishness.

"Who was that?" Olivia asked.

"Patrick, confirming tennis on Monday night."

"Well, dear, at least you know he wasn't involved in Mrs Valentine's disappearance. Maybe he's just as nice as you said he was."

"I guess I'll find out. I may as well keep seeing him for

now. Maybe he'll grow on me when I get to know him better."

Olivia frowned. "But he's good-looking. What's not to like?"

I raised my brow at her, and Ma'am actually smirked. "Olivia, dear, the only thing wrong with him, and every other man on the planet, is that he's not William."

My mouth dropped open as she turned and walked out of the room. My brain couldn't get it together in time to say something in my defence. If my feelings were obvious to everyone else, they were surely obvious to William, and he'd chosen to ignore them, so that gave me an answer. Of course, his relationship with Piranha was also a dead give-away that I didn't stand a chance, but I was stupidly stubborn like that.

It was definitely a good thing I had a date with Patrick. I knew I wasn't super attracted to him, so maybe he'd be a good rebound. What a joke. You were supposed to have a rebound from a relationship, but I'd had nothing with William except a pathetic crush. The sooner I could get over it and just see him as a friend, the better.

"Hey, fancy a game of chess?" Olivia looked at me and smiled.

"Okay. That's random, but why not. I haven't played in years, though, so go easy."

She cackled like an evil witch.

"Hey, that's how I'm supposed to laugh." I shook my head and gave her a dirty look, but then I ruined it by laughing.

We played two games. I lost both. Olivia obviously ignored my pleas to go easy... or maybe not, and I was really just that bad at chess. Either way, I was ready to call it a night. "Hey, want to go to Churchill's house tomorrow?"

"Yeah, sure. But will Angelica be okay with it?"

"I'll call her." I grabbed my phone off the table and called.

"Hello, Lily? Why are you phoning me?"

"I was just wondering if it was okay if Olivia and I went to Costa for breakfast tomorrow morning, then Churchill's place for a visit?"

"No, dear."

"No?" Hot tears stung my eyes. It was a total overreaction, I knew, but it made me feel trapped and frustrated.

"You didn't let me finish. I meant to say that I wasn't asking the reason for the call but why were you calling me rather than coming up to my room and knocking on my door."

"Oh." I was such an idiot. "I thought you'd gone back to work."

"No. I'm home for tonight, unless there's an emergency."

I tried not to get my hopes up again and braced for disappointment. I was an adult for goodness' sake. Setbacks were part of life, and I needed to just deal. "So, can we go? We'll be back by lunchtime." Except having to ask permission to go out made me feel like I was twelve.

"Yes, it should be fine. We just closed another case

yesterday, so I can spare two agents to watch out for you, but make sure you're back by twelve."

"Thanks, Fairy Godmother. Will do." I grinned.

"I can turn you into a pumpkin, you know."

"I don't doubt that. I'll make sure I'm back on time."

"Goodnight, dear."

"Night, Ma'am."

And that was that. Tomorrow was going to be awesome. Or maybe not.

THE NEXT DAY STARTED OFF WELL—BLUE SKIES AND NOT TOO cold. Top temperature today was going to be boiling hot at twenty-two Celsius. Okay, I was being sarcastic, but if I knew the English—which I felt I did a bit by now—they would be on the village green in their underwear sunning themselves and hoping to go a darker shade of white.

Olivia and I enjoyed a scrumptious breakfast of my favourite combination: cappuccino and chocolate muffin. Afterwards, we walked home, got in her car, and drove to Chartwell, Churchill's home. The nerves began when we got in the car, and by the time we'd arrived and parked, my hands were sweating, and I was having heart palpitations. I hadn't told Olivia about my mum's diaries yet. James and I agreed we should wait until she was a fully fledged member of the PIB first because she'd be helping us do some research. Knowing about the diaries might make her a target of the ones who were after me. They may try and magic her into finding the diaries and taking them. There was no way I could let that happen.

My parents had visited here just before they vanished, and I wanted to know why. Maybe my pictures could give me a clue. I hadn't told James, but if this panned out how I hoped it would, I was going to visit all the places in Mum's diary and take photos. Maybe I could piece together who was after them, or even what happened to my parents.

Knowing I may "see" my parents again today scared the crap out of me, but at least I was prepared this time, not like when I was in London and had a breakdown. There would be no bawling or vomiting—at least I hoped not. I'd had enough of vomiting, especially after yesterday.

Nervous energy bounced through my veins like a manic pinball. I gazed around at everything once we were out of the car, wondering exactly where my parents had walked. I was also worried about my plan being discovered by those who wanted me, but hopefully, they just thought I was here sightseeing. I was going to have to be careful about where I went and when. I'd need a good excuse for every visit, or whoever wanted my magic might decide to wipe me out quickly rather than risk discovery.

We headed to the visitor centre, bought tickets, and paid for parking. Looked as if they weren't relying on just the gift shop to pay for this one.

"Damn, Liv. The house doesn't open until 11:30. I'm only going to get about twenty minutes to look around before we have to leave."

"What happens if we're a bit late?"

"I turn into a pumpkin."

She laughed. I didn't. Being orange and filled with pulp and seeds didn't interest me in the slightest.

"The gardens are lovely, though. We'll have a good old wander."

"Yes, we will." I smiled, not wanting her to think I was upset. I wasn't really, just preoccupied. "At least it's nice weather." Without explaining myself, I took photos of the car park. If she thought I was weird, she didn't say anything. I whispered, "Show me my parents the last time they were here." A blue-sky day appeared through my lens, and I almost thought nothing had changed, until I realised the parked cars had changed. And there they were, my mum laughing at something Dad had said, while he stood holding her car door, waiting for her to get out. My heart wanted to break open and bleed grief all over the place, but I bit my tongue and willed the fissure to stay closed.

My dad had never been a showy kind of guy, but they'd arrived in what looked like a new black Porsche. I quickly peeked over my camera and ensured I wasn't about to walk in front of a car or into anyone. Then I approached the empty space where they'd been and took a picture of the number plate. Once that was done, I turned my camera off, ready to go to the next place. I was not going to take close-ups of their faces—that was just asking for a meltdown.

"Let's start." Olivia smiled.

We ambled along a path that led to the golden orfe pond. Green and red-leafed trees ringed the large pond, branches splaying over the water. Large orange fish swam around lazily, their scales bright against the murky green pond depths. I turned my camera on and pointed it at the one timber chair perched at the water's edge.

"Churchill used to sit there contemplating life and feeding his fish." Olivia's voice seemed to come from far away as I was wrapped up in the golden threads of magic.

"Show me my parents." Nothing. Maybe they didn't linger here, or maybe this wasn't the important part? "Show me Churchill." An overweight man appeared in the chair, leaning over, hand outstretched. A piece of bread fell from his hand, suspended forever in midair. His thin covering of grey hair was brushed back neatly, and a line ran vertically from his forehead to the top of his nose, a deep crease, evidence of a life spent worrying and thinking. I lowered the camera. This photo was definitely one for the history books. I'd have to show Millicent and Ma'am—they'd probably be quite interested.

We moved onto Lady Churchill's rose garden. As we walked the path between hundreds of rose flowers, their potent fragrance demanded my attention. I briefly closed my eyes to enjoy their scent. Once we reached the far side, I turned and took a few creative photos before asking to see my parents. Again, they were absent. Disappointment was like a vine, choking my hope. It was so very hard to see them, but now I realised it was worse not seeing them.

The main house, a three-storey Victorian building of orangey-brown bricks, chimneys, and large, many-paned windows, stood behind the garden. Unfortunately, we couldn't go in yet. "Where to now?"

"I think we'll—"

An alarm sounded, the noise a sharp stab to my eardrums. I clapped my hands over my ears. Olivia's mouth was still moving, but I couldn't hear her. And she was looking at me funny.

"Can't you hear that?" I shouted.

Her mouth moved, but I still couldn't hear what she was saying.

"The alarm!"

She shook her head, her eyes wide. A couple of elderly garden visitors stared at me, their expressions horrified at my outburst. Even their terrier had his head tilted as if to say, "Keep that woman away from me."

Oh, crap. Vlad's—the thug I killed in France—brother must have set off the magic alarm. I tried to ignore the blaring in my head and scanned my surroundings. He'd just entered the rose garden, approaching from the way we'd come. My eyes widened, and I turned to flee, but there was no way I could outrun him—not if he was using magic. I'd have to stay and fight. My thoughts were tumbling, tripping, a mess and unusable with my panic and the blaring siren, but a memory from my training broke through.

Use your other sight. I quickly dipped into the river. His aura showed only one defence spell—return-to-sender. I wasn't a gun person, but right now, I could have used one. I quickly put up a return-to-sender defence, and only just in time. He flicked his hand forward, and a spell hit me, sending me stumbling back. Whatever it was bounced off my defences and returned to him. He waved his arm and sparks flared, dissipating. What the hell had just happened?

I didn't have contemplation time as he lifted his arm again. Crap. Well, I'm sorry, PIB, but stuff the spectators. Angelica could wipe their minds later. I came up with a spell on the spot. "Grit on the ground, jump up and a new home you will find in Vlad's brother's nostrils and mouth." I didn't have time for rhyming, dammit.

The grit floated up from the path and swirled around his head before flying into his nose and mouth. He swatted his hands, trying to hit the rock granules away, but they were persistent little buggers, and they just kept coming. His mouth was jammed closed, and he'd covered his nose, but the little bits had already gone in, and I was pretty sure he was having trouble breathing. This was confirmed when he fell to his knees. He raised his head, anger and panic warring in his expression.

"Lily! Get down!" a man shouted. Two male agents entered the garden area at a run, both with guns raised and pointed at Vlad's brother. Now they show up? I could have been killed before they got here. What good was a security detail if they were too far away to see what was going on?

"Lily!" Déjà vu, anyone?

I turned. Ma'am was running from the house, Beren close behind. The PIB must have a landing place in there. I wondered if they'd had one there in Churchill's time? Had he been a witch?

"Are you okay, dear?" She gave me the once-over, and I felt a tingle, which meant she was probably checking me with her other sight as well. Beren raced to Vlad and ripped his arms away from his face before dragging them behind his back and slapping cuffs on him. Vlad fell forward as more stones embedded in his nostrils and mouth.

Beren looked up at me. "Lily, stop!"

I blinked. Stop? I'd never had to stop a spell before. They normally ran out in twenty-four hours or were an immediate one-use only.

Vlad's brother had stopped moving. Both the male agents looked at me with stern expressions. Was I in trouble?

Ma'am must have realised what was happening. "Just tell it to stop, Lily. Say, the last spell I cast, stop now because I ask."

I repeated the words. The frenzy of white and grey granules dropped as one, becoming harmless path once again. Beren knelt next to Vlad's brother and put his fingers to the man's throat. After a few seconds, he looked up and shook his head, then stood.

"Oh, shit, Lily. You killed him."

I looked at my friend, whose eyes were wide. "Thanks for the confirmation, Liv."

She bit her lip. "Sorry, I'm just... I've never seen a dead body before."

"I know. I'm sorry too. Of course you're shocked. Don't mind me." I was turning into a murderer. I'd killed two people. Did that make me a serial killer? And I knew it was all in self-defence, but it didn't change the outcome.

She put her hand on my shoulder, and I put my hand on

hers. "Thanks, Liv. I didn't mean to kill him. It was the first thing I could think of that wouldn't bounce back."

"What?"

"He had a return-to-sender spell, and I don't know enough to combat that. I just threw up my own return-to-sender spell and basically threw rocks at him. I figured the rocks weren't magic, that I was only moving them with magic, so they wouldn't come back to attack me. Turns out, I was right."

"It's okay, dear. You did the right thing, but now we can't interrogate him. We should've gotten here quicker. I was in a meeting with Pemberton, and he wouldn't let us leave immediately." Her glare and clenched teeth said it all.

"I'll leave you to sort this out." Beren bent and grabbed the dead guy's shoulder. Then they both disappeared.

"I suggest you two go home. I'll take care of the spectators." Both older ladies were frozen, as if they'd had a spell performed on them. Their mouths were open wide, arms slack by their sides. I was surprised neither of them had a heart attack.

As Ma'am approached the women, Liv and I walked to the car. I was cursed to be the only person who never made it to the gift shop at the end. I supposed it could be worse.

Yeah, right.

Olivia and I drove home, followed at a distance by the judgemental agents. Okay, so I didn't know for sure they were horrified by my lack of finesse and the fact that I'd just accidentally killed someone.

We watched Netflix for a while, and Olivia had a few

questions for me. I gladly answered them, but then we were both drained. The magic I'd used to defend myself had tired me out, and she had an exam on Monday. We'd just said goodnight, and my foot was on the first stair when Ma'am burst through the reception-room door.

Her gaze landed on me, serious yet more intense than normal. "Lily, we've had some news."

My heart rate kicked up. Oh, God, what now? "Has something happened to James?" I held my breath.

"No, dear. They've found Mrs Valentine's body, in the woods near her house. But she hasn't been there long, or the wild foxes would have started on her. Looks like it was only dumped there last night or this morning."

My stomach somersaulted as I remembered the gory image of her face down on the hotel room floor. "So what happens now? And what about the fact that Patrick was rifling through her desk." Would they ever catch Henry? And what had Patrick been looking for? There was more I should do, but I just wasn't sure what it was. I didn't like unanswered questions. How could Henry so easily get away with it, even though we knew it was him? Despair stomped my hope into the ground like a used cigarette butt and then twisted its unforgiving foot until it was well and truly embedded.

They'd never find him, and I may never know what part, if any, Patrick played. His going through her drawers may have been totally unrelated, but still.

"We'll conduct an autopsy, but other than that, nothing. I have agents combing the place she was found, but we won't need you yet. We already know who did it, and we have everyone looking for him. And as far as Patrick is concerned, maybe he's a petty thief? Whatever he was doing doesn't seem to be tied up in her murder, so we're going to let it go." She gave me a small smile. "Now you can go and get some sleep. You've had a big day."

I snorted. She was kidding, wasn't she? I would have almost been able to sleep, but then she went and dropped that on me, plus I was going to wonder what the hell Patrick had been doing. Did I want to spend my time with a poten-tial thief now that the case was over? Explaining would achieve nothing, so I just said, "Thanks for letting me know, and thanks for helping me today. Goodnight."

"Goodnight, ladies."

Olivia followed me up the stairs. I was pretty sure I could speak for both of us when I said it was far from a good night. What a hellish day. And I didn't even have a Chartwell fridge magnet to show for it.

CHAPTER 18

It was Monday afternoon. This morning had been slightly harrowing. I'd been called into the PIB to give a statement about what had happened yesterday. Because I'd acted in self-defence and hadn't meant to kill him, I was let off with a warning. Even Drake couldn't argue, since Will and Beren confirmed Vlad's brother had tried to kill me before. He was a wanted witch because of that. Drake did tell me not to kill anyone else, or I could find myself in jail. I needed to get on top of my magic and learn to disable attacking witches rather than finish them off.

Now I had to refocus on tennis. I wasn't sure what one wore to play tennis with rich British people, but I imagined it was supposed to be something dignified yet sporty. The day had been sunny and hot—by British standards, although at twenty-six degrees, it was actually comfortable weather for T-shirt and shorts, which is what I wore. I was risking things by wearing white shorts, but hey, what was a little more excitement?

Yesterday, the papers had done a spread on Mrs Valentine, her artwork, and the horrible tragedy of her partner murdering her. They used a picture of her and Knight. I'll admit I cried just a bit, and more for Knight than Mrs Valentine. I knew that sounded wrong, but I had gotten to know Knight a little bit, and he was a fairly defenceless animal, at least against witches. He wasn't going to hurt anyone by being alive. Unless he knew something about Henry he was going to tell us. I sighed. Now we'd never know.

My picture had been returned and hung above my bed. The PIB ruled it was Henry's magic signature on the painting because it matched the magic signature in her hotel room. They'd also confirmed it wasn't Mrs Valentine's signature first by going to her brother's. Apparently she'd exploded a teacup with magic the other day when they'd argued, and the residual magic was still in the room.

I still couldn't believe Henry had killed her for the money—her paintings were worth a lot more now that she was dead. And yes, that meant the one I had was worth more—Patrick said it might even be worth five times what I paid for it—but I wasn't going to sell it. Apart from the fact I liked it—even when the spell was taken away—I wanted it as a reminder of Ida and Knight. Anyway, she'd only left Henry five paintings—hardly worth killing for, surely? There must be more to it.

I grabbed my racquet, well, Ma'am's racquet. I walked

into the sitting room, where she was having a cup of tea. "I'm ready to go. Thanks for driving me to the gallery." I'd wanted to walk, but Ma'am insisted I be driven for safety reasons. Patrick was going to take us to the courts from there.

Angelica made no move to rise. "Yes, dear, you do look ready." She took another sip of tea.

What the? "Are you still driving me?"

She blinked. "No, not me." There was a noise from the hallway, and her gaze wandered past me. "Here's your lift. Right on time." She smiled.

I sagged. She'd be the death of me. Now I felt old. Wasn't that something you said about your child? I turned and would have sagged further if it didn't mean I'd be on the floor.

"Hey, sis." James was dressed in, dare I say it, tennis gear. And so was his companion… William.

"What are you doing?"

"Is that the thanks I get for giving you a lift and keeping an eye on you?" He raised a brow.

"You mean, you're going to play with us? But you can't. You weren't invited."

"We booked the court next door." William shrugged, as if it wouldn't drive me crazy to have him playing next to us. And what if this had been a proper date? There's no way I'd want them there, spying on me.

"I don't think that's a good idea. Didn't you question Patrick and his parents? They'll know who you are."

"Yes, but they won't know we're with you." James put his

arm around my shoulders. "After what happened at Chartwell, I'm not leaving anything to chance, Lily. Not until I can trust this idiot will look after you properly. Things can happen so quickly. Your well-being is not up for discussion."

Idiot? Wow, Patrick was up against it. Lucky for him, he probably wasn't that into me anyway. He didn't need my brother judging him and breathing down his neck. I really had to learn more magic; then no one would have to look out for me. Gah. "Right, well, don't give away that you know me. What if I want to actually date him now that the case is solved?"

"You mean you didn't really like him?" James dropped his arm and regarded me.

Argh, now I was going to have to admit to my stupidity in going "undercover" to try and catch someone who was innocent, at least of murder. "I thought I might be able to get more information out of him than you guys, since he didn't know I was with the PIB. But he's kind of cute, so why not go on a few dates, get to know him?"

Will's eye ticked. "I'm going to wait in the car. Hurry up, or you'll be late." He turned and strode out. James smirked as he watched his friend leave. I gave up.

"Come on, James. Will's right for once. I don't want to be late."

They dropped me around the corner from the gallery, at Westerham Hall, and I walked the rest of the way. The gallery was much busier than the last time I was in. Four people meandered in the first room, but Patrick was nowhere to be seen. I wandered into the next room where a crowd of about ten people stood in a semicircle, the ones at the back trying to see over other heads.

What were they looking at? I got closer. A nude in the same style as mine. I didn't need to look at the signature to know it was Mrs Valentine's. A short, slim woman in a navy-blue suit approached me. Her bleach-blonde hair was cut in a bob and blow-dried to within an inch of its life. It reminded me of straw. "Are you here to see Ida's painting?"

"Ah—"

"Well, you have some competition, I'm afraid. The auction is Thursday night, and we've had offers over fifteen thousand already. We're getting offers from all over Europe. This painting, and her others, are going to be very well known, I daresay. She's already famous in some circles." She smiled, demurely but contained. Wouldn't want to break out into an evil grin and start rubbing your hands. That wouldn't look good.

My eyes widened. *Fifteen thousand pounds*? Dying really did make you more important. Looked as if Henry stood to make some nice cash, but if he only had five paintings, what would that make it? Seventy thousand or more? I still didn't get it.

"Um, no. I'm just here to see Patrick. We're playing tennis this evening."

Her businesslike manner instantly changed, and she smiled. "Oh, you must be Lily! Lovely to meet you. I'm Patrick's mother, but you can call me Pamela."

"Thanks, Pamela. And lovely to meet you too. I hope you don't mind me crashing your game."

"Not at all. It's been a while since Patrick's brought home a lovely young lady. We're more than happy to have you join us. He hasn't stopped talking about you all weekend."

I grinned. How sweet. Although, he'd probably be mortified to hear what his mother was saying. "See that picture?"

"Yes."

"The young man has a lovely physique, doesn't he?"

"Mm, yes." It actually looked like the same man that was in my picture. This one was of his back, painted from the perspective of the other side of the bed. He was sitting on the bed, feet probably on the floor where we couldn't see, and he was stretching, arms bent and in the air, his back muscles bunched, defined. I looked around for Patrick, hoping to be saved from a slightly creepy conversation with his mother.

"That's Patrick. He's quite the catch, no? He'll be just as famous as Ida's paintings one day." She tilted her chin up and smiled.

Oh my God! I had Patrick's half-naked body hanging above my bed? I blushed. And he knew I liked it. Even without that stupid spell, I liked it. I took a deep breath. "Yes, he's quite the catch."

"Lily!" Saved by the subject. Patrick stopped next to his mother and smiled. "I hope Mother hasn't been bothering you." He looked at her, and his smile disappeared. Then he put his hand on my upper arm and bent down to kiss me on the cheek.

"No, not at all. She actually told me you're in this painting. I'm guessing the one I have in my room is you as well?"

He blushed but looked proud at the same time. "Yes, but I don't like to tell people."

"Did you ever model for her classes or just for her?" Something flashed through his eyes momentarily, but then it was gone. "Both."

"Shame you weren't the model when I did the class." I smiled and blushed. Did I really just say that? Oops.

He grinned. "I'm sure it could be arranged." He waggled his brows, and his mother shook her head. "That's enough, Patrick. Why don't you go and get changed? I'll get Prudence to finish up here. My things are in the car. I'll see you two there."

I smiled. "Bye."

Patrick kissed her cheek, and she left. "Sorry about that. She's more proud and pushy than she should be."

"She's your mum. She's supposed to be."

He looked at the door to the other room, frowning. "Some parents don't know when to stop."

Well, this was uncomfortable. I didn't know him well enough to be having this conversation, but he obviously needed to vent, or he wouldn't be telling me. I looked down at my sneakers. I hoped they were allowed on the court, as they had pink and blue soles, not white.

He slid his hand down my arm and linked his fingers with mine. It was... nice. Not setting off masses of butterflies, like with William, but there were a couple lazily bumping around in there. "I can get changed there. My clothes are in the car. I see you brought a racquet."

"Yep. Angelica had one lying around. So, we ready to roll?"

"Sounds good."

The drive out there only took five minutes. There was only one other car in the car park—Agent Crankypants's Range Rover. Would Patrick think it was weird if he noticed him, since he'd questioned him? This was never going to work. What if Patrick accused me of spying? But he wouldn't. He didn't know I knew Will and James. It could just be a massive coincidence. And besides, I wasn't really spying anymore, was I?

"Wait there." Patrick grabbed his bag from the back seat, got out, and came around my side to open the door. I couldn't help smiling again—chivalry and manners were so underrated. I enjoyed being treated as if I was important.

We walked around the clubhouse building to the back where two hard courts sat side by side. Both courts were vacant. Maybe William and James had decided to stay in the car until we were playing—their entrance would be less obvious. It was a pretty setting, the court area bordered by trees on the other side of the wire fence. There was even a weeping willow.

"Put your stuff down here." Patrick placed his bag on the ground next to the fence. I put my knapsack there and got my water bottle out to have a swig. It really was warm today. Yay for good weather.

Patrick then did something totally unexpected. He opened his bag, stood, and stripped his shirt off. He was facing me, and there was nothing for me to do but look at his well-formed chest. He grinned. So many things were running through my head, and I felt I should say something, if only to show I wasn't flustered because it was just a chest after all, even if it was sexy. But all I could come up with was a lip lick. Epic fail. His grin widened.

When he'd decided he'd tortured me enough, he slipped his blue-collared T-shirt over his head. Just before he slipped it down, I realised what had been niggling at my brain since I'd bought the painting.

Was that a heart-shaped mole just above his nipple? Didn't Henry have one in the same spot? Well, that was weird. But I hadn't gotten a good enough look.

Now Patrick was taking off his polished brown work shoes and dropping his work pants. My mouth dropped open. His white legs were on show, and while they weren't bad to look at, I didn't need to see his boxers on the second date, or was it our third? Who did that? Who just undressed where anyone could see? And he had white briefs on. Ew. That was like me getting caught with my granny undies on. Not a good look.

He must have noticed my horrified expression. "Chill, Lily. I'm keeping my underpants on." He laughed. Oh, that's right, he nude modelled on the side. But in this instance, maybe it would have been better if he'd taken those undies off. This probably felt like being overdressed to him. I smiled and shrugged. Just because I wasn't confident enough to publicly and randomly undress myself while wearing ugly underwear—or even beautiful underwear for that matter—didn't mean those who were okay with it were weird. Not. At. All. Move this to the beach, and it would be totally acceptable, although still not sexy.

Once he was dressed, he grabbed my hand and pulled me close. "Thanks for coming, Lily." He was staring into my eyes. Oh, crap. Now I knew why his eyes seemed familiar, and it wasn't because we were destined to be together. He had the same eyes as Henry. I would swear my life on it. Was Henry his father? No, that was too weird. And I still had to check the mole again. But how?

"Are you okay?"

"Ah, yeah, sorry. I was just freaking out because my tennis is so bad. I hope I don't end up making a terrible impression."

"You could never make a terrible impression." He kissed my forehead; then someone behind us coughed.

I turned to see James and William walking to their court, which was next to ours. "Good afternoon," said James. William just gave a wave, and I almost choked. He was wearing a long black beard and sunglasses. That must be a disguise. I snorted as quietly as I could.

"Let's have a warm-up before your parents get here."

"Okay." Patrick grabbed some balls and jogged to the other side of the court, leaving me to figure out how he and Henry could be related. I'd never met his father. Maybe his father was Henry, but Henry had disappeared so he was unlikely to turn up here. Or maybe his father was Henry's brother? I mean, Patrick couldn't *be* Henry; could he? That was impossible. Right? Same eyes, same birthmark... maybe. But that was only my opinion. And I'd admit I was wrong sometimes... cough.

But now that the idea was in there, it wasn't coming out.

The first ball sailed over the net. I drew my arm back and kept my eye on the ball. Amazingly, I did an okay forehand. It went back over the net, although Patrick had to run to the middle of the court to return it. As we warmed up, I pondered how to find out if he and Henry were the same person. I ignored the voice in my head saying I was a total nutcase and imagining things.

If I was going to figure this out, I needed to do it before his parents got here. I turned and looked towards the car park. No one was walking from there, so I was in the clear. "Hang on." I held up my hand and jogged to his side of the court.

"You know, Lily, for this to work, we have to be on opposite sides of the net." He laughed.

"I know. It's just..." I bit my lip. I'd never been great at flirting or being forward with men, but this was important. I looked into his eyes and put my hand on his chest, then curled my fingers around the V at the top of his shirt and started pulling.

His eyes widened, and he wrapped one arm around my waist. "I'm not saying I'm against this, but what are you doing?"

"After hearing it's you in the drawing in my room, I need to see your chest again. Like, right now. I have a thing for pecs." I tried not to laugh. Hmm, I wasn't far off the truth; however, I'd never ever say it to a guy, except in dire circumstances.

"You can see my chest any time you like."

He took his arm from around my waist and took his shirt off. Just like that. Wow, getting guys naked was way too easy. If I'd known all this time how easy it was, maybe I would have had more action.

For this to be believable, I was going to have to go for it. I put my palm on the non-mole side of his chest—which was warm and firm. Mmm. And slightly squishy if I grabbed— *No, Lily. Bad, Lily.* Focus on the mole.

This is what happened when you didn't date enough.

I cleared my throat and took a good look at his nipple. Was I really doing this? The mole was the same size, shape, and position from what I remembered of Henry's. Patrick lowered his mouth to my ear and whispered, "You're so hot. Wanna come back to my place later?"

Something thumped me on the head. "Ow!" I rubbed my scalp. I turned in time to duck the second ball. What the hell?

"Oops." That was not the tone of an apologetic man, more like a sarcastic one. "Sorry to interrupt, but can we have our balls back please?" William was up our end but on his court, not even twenty metres away. He stared at us, hands on hips, and although I couldn't see his eyes with those dark sunglasses on, I knew he was glaring.

I bit the inside of my cheek to stop from smiling. Was he jealous? I looked up at Patrick. "I guess you can put your shirt back on. I'll get the balls." I jogged to retrieve them, then hit them back... badly, on purpose. I hit them in the far corner of their court so William would have to walk to get them. As much as I didn't really want to make out with Patrick, especially now that I knew he might be Henry—the idea of him really being a wrinkly old guy was ridiculously off-putting—who I made out with was none of Will's business, and he shouldn't be interfering.

He managed a "thanks."

"My pleasure, but next time, keep your balls to yourself. We have enough on this side of the court. Thank you."

He stared at me for a moment longer, then grunted. James snickered.

Patrick, shirt on, came over. "Wow, you were hard on that guy. I'm sure it was an accident."

I smiled. "Was I? I didn't notice. Okay, let's get back to it." I went back to my side of the court.

After another five minutes, Patrick's parents turned up. If his father *was* Henry, there was no doubt Will and James would arrest him as soon as they realised. Adrenaline flooded my body as I waited for his father to get close enough for me to see what he looked like. What would be worse—him being Henry or not? If he wasn't, then it could still be Patrick, assuming my theory was correct. But how? How could someone look like someone else, and Henry was old, like forty years older than Patrick, and he'd had sex with Mrs Valentine. I shuddered.

"Hello, Son." His dad had sunglasses on. He waved at

Patrick, then approached me. "You must be Lily. Lovely to meet you."

He was wearing aviator sunglasses, but he was tall, at least six three, and Henry was shorter—a similar height to Patrick. His dad also had a potbelly, something Henry didn't have, and a hooked nose, thinning hair. Like the man who had tampered with Knight's food? I was pretty sure if I'd asked to see his bare chest, he wouldn't have a heart-shaped mole, and I'd come off looking like an even bigger weirdo than I felt. But maybe he was the one who killed Knight.

"Lovely to meet you too." I shook his hand. When I let go, I was still looking at his hand. My mouth dropped open. He was wearing the same gold ring from the photo I'd taken that day at Mrs Valentine's. He had to have been the one who tampered with Knight's food.

His mother jogged up to us, racquet in hand. "You go play with Pat, and we'll stay up this end."

I blinked, trying to get myself together. "Okay." I ran back to the other side of the court and glanced at William, who had paused his serve to watch me. If only I could tell him to go away. Gah.

By the time the two hours of tennis was up, I still hadn't figured out how to solve my problem. After seeing Patrick's dad's ring, it was more likely than ever Patrick was Henry. But I still couldn't see how that was possible. I could just outright ask Patrick, but if I were wrong, he'd figure I was crazy, and if I were right, he would probably kill me too and run. Crap.

As he drove me home, I stole glances of his face. High

cheekbones, warm brown eyes, long lashes. How could he be a killer? He looked like a big softy, albeit one who was immature at times, but then, Henry had looked like a softy too. I'd have to talk to Angelica. There was no way I was going to figure this out by myself.

He opened my car door when we got home, and I climbed out. We stood face-to-face.

"Thanks so much for this afternoon. I had fun." And I kind of had, apart from the shock of seeing the mole and his dad's ring. Did that make me a bad person?

"Me too. And my parents love you. I can tell. You sure you don't want to come back to my place?" He grinned.

"I'm actually all tuckered out after tennis," I lied. "But maybe next time. I guess I'll see you soon." I smiled.

"I'll call you." This time, the kiss on the cheek never came. He put both arms around me and planted a warm, lingering kiss on my lips. It was okay, until I pictured old, wrinkly Henry. Ew. And who was the real person—Henry or Patrick? God, I felt as if I was losing it, big time.

"Bye, Patrick." I turned and went inside. I shut the door and stood in the vestibule until the hum of his engine faded. Things still didn't add up. I couldn't reconcile that young man with Henry the Murdering Bastard. And if they were one and the same person, why? Why would you do it? I could understand an older person wanting to look young, but what about his parents? Did that make them over one hundred? No, that couldn't be right. Witches could do magic, not miracles.

"Lily. What are you doing there?" Angelica stood in

front of me. How long had she been standing there while I'd been in my own world?

"I just got home from tennis, and I have a problem." I could totally run this past Angelica. She'd tell me if I was being stupid.

"By the look on your face, this could take a while. Come and sit." We walked into the sitting room, to the Chesterfields. "So…"

"Yes, so. This is going to sound crazy." I pressed my lips together.

"It's probably not as crazy as you think. When you've lived as a witch for as long as I have, you realise almost nothing's impossible."

And that's what worried me.

I told her everything, from the time I'd seen Henry's mole to today, even about my suspicion that Patrick's dad had killed Knight. She'd nodded slowly at some points, made a few "I'm listening" noises, but at no point did she say I was nuts. I guessed she'd seen some out-there stuff in her time.

"So, is it possible?"

"Yes. Not probable, but possible. There is a spell to change how you look, but it takes a huge amount of skill and energy. It's a glamour spell, but the person would look, sound, and feel different once they were changed, although some things would stay the same because it would take too much power to change everything. In this case, his eyes and that mole."

"Is there an easy way to find out, or do we need to get

him to do magic and test his signature?" Guilt tapped me on the shoulder and asked if I was done betraying my potential future boyfriend. Even if he wasn't Henry, there was no way I could keep dating him after what I'd thought. He didn't deserve someone like that, someone he couldn't trust. And I knew we weren't really going anywhere in the long-term. I wasn't over Will, and I didn't know when I would be. Argh.

"I think that's an excellent idea, Lily. Maybe we should ask him over for dinner, so he can meet the closest thing you have to parents." She gave me a shy smile. "And while we're off-duty, you may call me Angelica. I think it's time we dropped some of the formalities. "What? Huh? Where had that come from? Moisture filled my eyes. To be fair, she had taken me by surprise. I cleared my throat. "That would be lovely. And I know Mum and Dad would appreciate it if they knew, and I do too. You've done so much for me since I arrived. So, thank you… Angelica." I smiled as that salty liquid leaked down my cheeks.

She leaned over and gave me a quick hug before sitting up straight and back to her normal composed, unemotional self. I loved that she'd broken out of her comfort zone, even if it had only been for a few seconds.

"So, I'll ask him to come around, and we'll get him to do some magic. I don't think it will be hard. He likes showing off." Something else occurred to me. "But what if his parents are involved? Those paintings have gone up in value, and even though Henry only had five, the art society ended up with the rest. How many, I have no idea, but there was a crowd looking at one today when I went to the gallery.

The value of her paintings has increased at least tenfold. They're marketing them as the work of a dead artist. Patrick's mum also said something about him being the subject of some of her paintings and that he'd be famous." I frowned. "I can't imagine he did this all by himself. He's not perfect, but he doesn't strike me as being that desperate for fame." I sighed loudly. "I just don't know. Maybe I'm tripping down the entirely wrong track?"

"Trust your instincts, dear. If your brain is telling you you've seen those eyes and that mole on Henry, you probably have. Now, just let me work everything out. All you'll have to do is ask him to dinner. Let me know when you have a day. Maybe try for Wednesday. If he is the killer, we don't want him out in the wide world longer than necessary. Maybe ask his parents to come too. I think if they're involved, it's best to have them here where we can round them all up at once."

"Okay." I swallowed my nerves. If I was wrong, this was going to be all kinds of embarrassing, and if I was right…. Lose, lose. Except Mrs Valentine would have a win, even if it was too late to save her and Knight. Why couldn't life be easy for a change? It was just one near disaster after another.

After another.

CHAPTER 19

It was Wednesday night. I couldn't believe it had been so easy to get Patrick and his parents here. My acting skills were obviously awesome. It was probably my guilt making me think they'd be suspicious something other than a get-to-know-you dinner was going on.

Patrick, Olivia, and I chatted while Angelica got to know Patrick's parents. Everyone except me had a glass of wine. I was cradling tap water. A Baileys would have been nice, but I needed to keep a clear head. My magic and brain-to-mouth filter was bad enough when I was sober.

"I have to get the hors d'oeuvres out of the oven."

Patrick looked at me. "But you're a witch. Shouldn't you just, you know…" He waved his hand in the air.

"I'm not very good yet. I'm likely to drop them all."

Olivia giggled, and I shot her a cranky look.

"What? I was just agreeing with you."

I rolled my eyes, but then I grinned. Being angry with her was a lost cause, and I knew she was just having fun. "Do you mind helping me, Patrick?" I touched his arm—I'd heard that was a rule of flirting, to be touchy-feely. Not really my thing, but I'd try anything once. Well, almost anything—I would never ever, ever suck someone's toes. I shuddered.

He grabbed my hand. "Sure. Lead the way."

We went to the kitchen. I turned the oven off and opened the door. "There they are. Could you just magic them onto this platter pretty please? Ha, platter pretty please, platter pretty please, platter pretty please."

"What are you doing?" Patrick's face was devoid of anything that said "fun."

"Sorry. I like a good tongue twister. It was there, and I couldn't resist." I shrugged, then picked the white platter up off the table. "Would you do the honours, kind sir?"

"I can handle this. Step aside, young lass." He pushed his sleeves up with an exaggerated motion. This joking side of him was nice. I was going to be sad if he was Henry. It was still hard to believe Patrick could have killed Mrs Valentine. How could people seem so nice but be so evil? And how could I be such a betrayer? He magicked the food onto the large white dish, the little puff pastries forming neat lines. Now we had his magic signature on the food. Angelica would get one and send it to be tested.

"Thanks, Patrick. Maybe one day I'll be as good at magic as you."

"Just keep practicing." He winked.

I went back into the sitting room and offered the food around. Patrick's mum took one and bit into it. "Mmm. These are delicious. Thank you."

Angelica took one. "Thank you, dear." As she popped it into her mouth, I sneezed.

"Bless you," said Patrick's dad. I resisted glaring at him. I'd gone back and looked at the picture I'd taken of the man putting the spelled food into Knight's bowl, and with the ring, I was sure it was him.

"Thank you." I sniffed, trying to make it as believable as possible. When I'd sneezed, Angelica had magicked the pastry to James, who would be checking the magic signature against Henry's right now. I looked over at Patrick, who was laughing with Olivia. It was as if a giant centipede was Irish dancing in my stomach. If he was Henry, he was not going to be happy when we arrested him. And what would his parents do? I was fully prepared to protect Olivia, and I went and stood next to her, just in case.

Magic signatures were complex animals, so it would take a few minutes for James to confirm. In the meantime, sweat slid down the valley between my boobs. I pulled a face. Yuck. How was I supposed to deal with that? I pushed my shirt into the valley and tried to mop it up. Why was nervous sweat a thing? It was uncomfortable enough being nervous without leaking moisture and giving a person more to worry about. Oh, God, did I have huge wet patches under my arms? I lifted one arm and then the other and looked.

Olivia stared at me. "What the hell are you doing?"

"I'm just a bit hot."

Patrick grinned and nodded.

He had to go there. Why did guys always have to go there? Sometimes it was best to just let those comments go. I wasn't in the mood for flirty banter, but I supposed he didn't know that.

Argh, I was such a bad sort-of girlfriend.

There was a knock on the front door. I tensed. Olivia and I shared a worried glance. That would be James. If Patrick's signature hadn't matched, he was going to send Angelica a text, but if it was positive, he was going to turn up like a normal person, to avoid startling the prey. He would also have other agents with him.

A prickly wave of disappointment and anger shredded its way through my veins. As Angelica answered the door, I couldn't help but look at Patrick, my feelings clear on my face. "Why?" I asked.

"Why what?" Then he must have realized what I was talking about. He was Henry, and he had known this whole time I worked with the PIB. Millicent and I had questioned him, for goodness' sake. But he must have believed he'd gotten away with it, let his guard down. All the colour seeped from his face; then red replaced the stark white as fury lit his fuse. "What are you talking about, Lily?" Wow, so he was going to try and pretend his way out of it.

James and Angelica entered, followed by Beren, William, Dana Piranha, and two other agents—the man and woman who watched over me the other day but whose names I couldn't remember. I was hopeless.

Dana gave me a dirty look—what the hell had I done?

—then she cuffed Patrick's dad before he could cast a spell. Beren cuffed Patrick's mum while James and Will approached Patrick.

After everything that had happened, I'd gotten to know him, and I wanted to hear what he had to say for himself. I also wanted answers for Knight and Ida. "Why did you do it, Patrick, or should I say, Henry?"

"You can't prove anything." He looked warily at James and stepped back until he hit the back of one of the armchairs next to the fireplace.

"Unfortunately, we can. Those hors d'oeuvres you helped me with; that's how."

"But what did I do, exactly? Help you. You're arresting me for helping you?"

He obviously had no idea we'd found her car or the hotel room. I couldn't give everything away, so I fibbed. "Someone reported her car had been sitting in the street… another witch, so the no-notice spell didn't work on them. It was your magic signature, Patrick. And that mole on your chest is just like Henry's. What I really want to know, well, one of the things I really want to know, is are you old, or is this your real form?" James, Will, and I stepped closer in unison, Will angling more around the other side of the chair. Patrick tried to look at us all at once, his eyes darting around.

His mother tried to walk forward, but Beren held her cuffed hands behind her back. "Don't tell them anything, Pat. Keep your mouth shut, and we can walk away with what's ours. And you." She stared daggers at me, and I had no doubt that if she had access to her magic, there would be something sticking out of my chest right now. "How can you live with yourself, betraying your boyfriend like that?"

My mouth dropped open. What? Out of everything that had happened, that's what she was focussing on? What a nutjob. "Maybe you should be asking yourself how Patrick could kill someone." I stared at him again, into those eyes that were his and Henry's. "So are you really Henry or Patrick?"

His eyes were pleading. "I'm as you see me now. Please, Lily. You can't believe I would kill anyone. I'm not Henry. I don't care what they say." He finished it off by looking at the ground, then sneaking glances around, probably to make sure he wasn't about to be cuffed.

Well, I had to give him points for perseverance. He was as stubborn as I was. "Why did you do it? Surely it wasn't all about the money. I don't know you well, but I know you enough to be confused as to why. Was it really about the money?"

Patrick's mother grunted. I looked over to see her still struggling against Beren's hold. "Patrick, if you ruin this for us, I'll kill you. Think of how hard you've worked over the last two years, what you've had to put up with. Don't let me down. I'll disown you."

His head slowly lifted. He stared at his mother, his eyes glassy. He looked like a deer that had just been shot by someone it trusted. He blinked a few times. "After everything I've been through, you'd disown me?"

She narrowed her eyes at him. "You're such a disappointment."

Patrick shook his head slowly. "I did all this for you, Mother. For you."

"Shut up, you dolt!" She turned to her husband. "Make him shut up for Christ's sake."

Patrick's father shook his head. "No, Pamela. I've gone along with your crazy schemes long enough. I've watched my son suffer, and I should've stepped in and stopped the whole farce long ago." He turned sad eyes on Patrick. "I'm sorry, Son. Can you forgive me?"

This was like an episode of *Days of Our Lives*. And I had no idea what they were talking about. What was going on?

"Farce? Farce?" Pamela's voice rose, until she was shouting. "This was for our family. Patrick was born to be a star, and we deserve that money. That hag took advantage, even when she knew the truth, but she couldn't agree to one little attraction spell. Not one. After everything we did for her." She lunged for her husband. Beren yanked her back, and she slammed against his chest. "You'll regret this, Simon. We'll be the laughing stock of the art world. If you don't back me in this, I'll never speak to you again." Was she growling? Ooh, there was a bit of froth too.

"Take her away for questioning, Agent DuPree."

"Yes, Ma'am."

"Don't you—" she shrieked at Patrick, her crazed eyes glowing with hate. But before she could finish, Beren dragged her through a doorway.

Patrick's shoulders sagged, and he held his arms out. "Just get this over with." James cuffed him.

"Patrick, please tell me what happened. I don't believe you're a cold-blooded murderer." Maybe I was a fool, but this beaten-down man in front of me with the sad brown eyes was damaged, and I hadn't even realised.

"I can't tell you, Lily. I'm ashamed. But please know I'm sorry... for everything."

He hung his head. James turned to me. "I have to take him now, Lily. Sorry."

I shrugged, as if to say, okay.

Piranha's voice was louder than it needed to be. "Come on, Will. Let's get this one back to headquarters, leave the idiot witch to get over her murdering boyfriend." I turned and stared at her. Wow, she wasn't even trying to be subtle. "Yes, Lily. You're an idiot. You're a useless witch. I have no idea why Ma'am keeps you around. But I'll work it out. Ta, ta." She raised her eyebrow at Will, then stepped through her doorway, taking Patrick's dad with her. The other two agents, the ones whose names I couldn't recall, followed her out.

Will looked at me, but I couldn't read what he was thinking. His cold, stern expression was on. He looked as if he might say something but then shook his head, made his doorway, and stepped through. Wow, way to stick up for me. Did he hate me for lying to Patrick? Or was he angry because he thought I'd been dating Patrick? Whatever it was, he let his girlfriend chomp me to shreds, as usual. Did I really need to know anymore?

Angelica met my gaze. "I'd bet my favourite grimoire that there's more to this story, Lily, and when I find out, I'll let you know."

I nodded. I wanted to ask her to go easy on Patrick, but what did I really know about him? Maybe he was trying to con me to the end, but his mother... what a witch. Had she driven him to it somehow? I had a feeling she was behind the whole thing, but I'd have to wait to get answers.

"I'll see you both later." Angelica disappeared.

I shuffled over to the Chesterfields and dropped into one. Olivia joined me. "Wow, that was... intense. Are you okay?" she asked.

Was I? I'd thought I wasn't getting attached, but there was a tiny ache in that thing I called a heart. He'd almost looked like a lost child when his mother was in full rant. But still, he'd killed Ida—I couldn't deny that—I'd seen it with my own eyes. As sad as I was, I knew catching him was the right thing to do. However, being undercover, pretending to have motivations I didn't, unsettled me. I had betrayed his trust, in more ways than one. And I'd confused myself. "I don't know. Ask me tomorrow, when I've had time to digest all this."

"Speaking of digesting, we didn't really get to eat. Do you think Angelica would mind if we polished off some of that Black Forest cake? It's not like we have any guests to feed." Her eyes glittered with caketicipation.

I gave her a sad smile. "You go ahead. I'm not really hungry right now."

"You sure?"

"Yeah. I'm sure."

Olivia got up and made her way to the kitchen. When she'd reached the door, I called out, "But leave me half."

She snorted. "Of course. What kind of friend would I be if I ate all the cake?"

"An ex-friend?"

She grinned and left the room.

I sat and stared sightlessly at the floor. Why did doing the right thing have to feel so wrong?

CHAPTER 20

I sat next to Millicent and glared across the conference room table at Piranha. Ma'am, at the head of the table, clapped. Everyone sat up straighter and looked at her.

"Good morning, team. I just wanted to say congratulations on a job well done. Another case solved." She saved a satisfied smile just for Drake, who kept his expression neutral, but he smoothed down his tie… three times. Maybe he was hoping a genie would appear and save him. I wasn't sure why, but he'd tried to sabotage her investigation. She'd come out victorious anyway. Yay, Ma'am!

Ma'am 1: The Duck: 0.

I smirked.

"I haven't just called you here to congratulate you. When we interviewed Patrick last night, he was very forthcoming with information. He admitted to murdering Mrs Valentine. His motive wasn't money. He was trying to please his mother, who wanted the prestige and money from the sale of the paintings, and from having her son known as the model in the paintings." Her gaze rested on me. "Patrick, it seems, paid a high price to deliver what his mother wanted. He had to date Mrs Valentine, but knowing she would never date someone so young—he was twenty-eight when this started—Patrick's mother insisted he take on the role of an older man. And Henry was born."

Bile rose in my throat. I swallowed the burn. "So, he was dating her, but he didn't like her?"

Slow clapping came from across the table. Piranha. "Give the girl a medal. Great powers of deduction, Lilith."

I breathed in. I was so going to give her an itch where the sun never shone. I checked she didn't have any spell protections, then whispered, "Give Dana an itch she can't ignore, in her—"

"Dana, leave Lily alone, please. Your behaviour is unprofessional." Huh. Will finally stuck up for me, even if it was a little bland and lacking emotion.

Her mouth dropped open, and she lifted a palm to her cheeks, as if he'd just slapped her. "I can't believe you'd take her side over mine!" How old was she again?

"There is no side. Lily's sitting there minding her own business."

I blushed and looked around. This was unprofessional, even if I hadn't started it. Piranha was making me look like a child, like someone who had to be defended by others. I needed to find my tongue and shut this down. I may not want to work here full-time, but I still had my pride. "Look, Dana, I have no idea why you hate me, and I really don't care, but unless you have something nice to say, I'm not interested. Your barbs don't bother me. When you've lost the people you love most in the world, everything else comes a really, really distant last place."

She glared at me but didn't answer. Then she turned and pouted at William. "I'll do this for you, Will. But only because I love you. Having her here makes this place look like a day-care centre. When I left for New York, this was a top-notch outfit. Now, I'm not so sure." She gave me a sideways glare.

I ignored her and turned to Angelica. "Please continue, Ma'am. I'd really like to know what else you found out."

"Thank you, Lily." She cocked her head to the side and regarded Dana. Hopefully she was finally noticing what a poisonous witch she had working here—best agent or not. "To keep the ruse going, he had to sleep with Ida, and he hated every second of it. His mother knew but didn't care. Eventually, Ida found out, but she was in love with Henry by then and insisted Patrick keep seeing her as Henry."

"What the hell? That's messed up. Why didn't he just stop?" I was horrified on his behalf. My feelings on Mrs Valentine were torn: she didn't set out to fall in love with him, but knowing he mustn't love her, wouldn't she want him out of her life? Or was she trying to punish him?

"Ida had proof Patrick and his parents were spelling her paintings, so they would sell more easily and for more. They also spelled them when they were in competitions so she'd win and get a good name. Ida was against cheating, but Pamela wouldn't hear of stopping. She had her heart set on her own goals. In the beginning, they targeted her because she had money, was a fairly good artist, but also wasn't attached to anyone. They saw an easily manipulated woman who they could control. They had exclusive rights to distribute and sell her work. But then Ida turned the tables and blackmailed them, forcing Patrick to keep seeing her."

James nodded. "And killing her took care of three problems. One, she wouldn't go to the police. Two, Patrick could stop seeing her, and three, the value of her paintings would skyrocket because she was dead."

I shuddered. The whole thing was disgusting. I knew he was guilty of terrible crimes, but how scarred would you be sleeping with someone who repulsed you and that your own parents prostituted you out to? He'd had no one to turn to. All he'd wanted was his mother's approval. That was just... I had no words. My nose tingled as tears burnt my eyes.

I took a deep breath. "That day he was in her office drawer, the time Knight told us about"—yikes, I had to be careful about what I said if I didn't want Piranha to find out about my talent—"what was he looking for? Did you find out?"

Ma'am swallowed and shifted. She cleared her throat. "Whilst she preferred Patrick as Henry, especially in public, she drew him as Patrick and sometimes preferred sleeping with him as such. She had a memory stick with many, many naked images of him. In some of them, she'd asked him to do questionable things to her, things he was extremely embarrassed about. He wanted to destroy that memory stick. The original plan had never been to kill Mrs Valentine, but Patrick finally snapped when she threatened to put the videos on the Internet, not to mention, he couldn't stand another minute in her bed."

What was wrong with some people? Mrs Valentine was just as crazy as Patrick's mother, and Patrick… what could I say about him? This ball of string was way too tangled to unravel. I didn't think I'd ever understand this situation in its entirety. The whole thing just made me want to cry.

Ma'am also told us Patrick's dad killed Knight so the fox wouldn't tell anyone about Patrick being Henry. Apparently, animals could see through glamours. There were a few more boring details to clear up, but finally, we finished. Everyone left, except James and William, much to the annoyance of Miss Piranha. I stood to leave, but William came around the table. "I just wanted to apologise, Lily. I know Dana can be… difficult—"

"That's the polite way of saying it." I folded my arms. I needed a barrier between us, and this was as good as I was going to get.

"Well, anyway, I'll make sure she doesn't bother you anymore. Okay?" His grey-blue eyes stared into mine, the intensity stealing my words. I hated myself for wanting to throw my arms around him and just breathe in his scent, forget how awful he'd been. But how much of an idiot would that make me?

"Yeah, okay, Will. But what happened with us? I thought we were friends. Now it's like the day we met, when you seemed like you hated me. What did I do wrong?"

He opened his mouth, sadness breaking through that tough veneer guarding his eyes, and my heart raced. Was he going to say something good or bad? Then he shut it again and shook his head. "We're friends, Lily. I'll always have your back. But right now, I have to get back to Dana." He turned to James and shook his hand. "See you tomorrow, man."

"See ya."

James and I watched him disappear, but I swore I could see the imprint of him as a negative in the space he'd just occupied, like when you look at a window during the day, then shut your eyes quickly. The impression it leaves behind stays with you. And stupid Will was still in my heart, like a bad case of nits you couldn't get rid of. I'd killed those feelings off just to have them multiply and come back in force, again and again. Yeah, unrequited love was totally lousy.

James gave me a hug. "I know this thing with Will is getting you down, but it will work out how it's supposed to. He just has things to figure out."

"It's okay. You don't have to make me feel better. It is what it is. I'll get over it, just maybe not till next century. You can't rush these things." I smiled despite my aching lice-infested heart.

He dropped his arms and stepped back to look at me.

"What are you going to do with that artwork? I'm not sure if I feel sorry for the guy or not. He did some terrible things, but he was obviously driven to it."

"I don't know about the picture. I'm not sure if I want to be reminded of his situation and Knight day after day. Maybe I'll sell it and donate the money to help abused kids. What chance did he have with a mother like that?"

"Too right. There was something else I wanted to tell you, but I can't do it here."

"About Mum and Dad?"

"Yes, and I'd like to hear how you're doing with… things." By things, I was sure he meant Mum's diaries.

"Yeah, sure. When?"

"Dinner at mine on Saturday night. You can bring Angelica if you like, and Olivia. I think it's time we got some help from someone else we can trust."

"Okay, big bro. I'll see you then."

"Bye, Lily."

I stepped through my doorway and into Angelica's reception room. The house was quiet. I knew what I had to do.

I made my way to the kitchen. There was half a Black Forest cake in the fridge, and it was all mine. I made a coffee to go with it, then settled at the table. I sniffed the heady scent of chocolate, cherries, and cream. Mmm. My mouth watered in caketicipation. Before I dug in, I raised my coffee mug. "Knight, I hope you can now rest in peace. You were the only truly innocent one in all of this. I'll never forget you."

From somewhere in the distance, or maybe it wasn't even in the mortal plane, came high-pitched keening. The hairs on the back of my neck stood on end. Was that a fox?

Tears welled in my eyes, and I smiled. Looks like I'd gotten to say goodbye to Knight after all.

ACKNOWLEDGEMENTS

Two fantastic editors worked on this book: Becky and Chryse. Thank you both for helping me improve this book. Thanks to Vesna for always wanting the next one. And I'd like to thank my brain for continuing to play along with this writing caper.

ABOUT THE AUTHOR

USA Today bestselling author, Dionne Lister is a Sydneysider with a degree in creative writing, two Siamese cats, and is a member of the Science Fiction and Fantasy Writers of America. Daydreaming has always been her passion, so writing was a natural progression from staring out the window in primary school, and being an author was a dream she held since childhood.

Unfortunately, writing was only a hobby while Dionne worked as a property valuer in Sydney, until her mid-thirties when she returned to study and completed her creative writing degree. Since then, she has indulged her passion for writing while raising two children with her husband. Her books have attracted praise from Apple iBooks and have reached #1 on Amazon and iBooks charts worldwide, frequently occupying top 100 lists in fantasy. She's excited to add cozy mystery to the list of genres she writes. Magic and danger are always a heady combination.

ALSO BY DIONNE LISTER

Paranormal Investigation Bureau

Witchnapped in Westerham #1

Witch Swindled in Westerham #2

Witchslapped in Westerham #4

Witch Silenced in Westerham #5

The Circle of Talia

(YA Epic Fantasy)

Shadows of the Realm

A Time of Darkness

Realm of Blood and Fire

The Rose of Nerine

(Epic Fantasy)

Tempering the Rose